KILLIAN

SUSIE MCIVER

BAND OF NAVY SEALS
KILLIAN
AUTHOR
SUSIE MCIVER

Cover Design by Emmy Ellis

❀ Created with Vellum

PROLOGUE

Killian was ten, when he went to the lake with his brother and other kids from the foster care system they all were in. The county brought them to the lake twice a year. Mostly only the people who lived on the lake had their boats on it, and the rich people who had their beautiful homes here allowed the foster kids to a day on the lake twice a year. This trip was the first time they got to ride in a boat. One of the workers at the foster home bought a boat for one hundred dollars. He was so proud of that boat. The kids were taking turns riding in it. Killian didn't want to ride in the boat, but his foster sister Emma told him he had to ride and quit acting like a child. Killian got in the boat even though he didn't want to. He was mad at Emma for saying he was a baby. When they were far out on the lake, something happened. Killian could smell gas. He wasn't waiting around for the boat to catch on fire. As he dove into the lake, the boat exploded.

When Killian woke up, he was with an older couple. He couldn't remember anything. They told him he was their son Brice Allan. Killian couldn't remember if that was true or not. When his parents brought him home after the boating accident, they were all surprised at how good a swimmer he was. He could stay under for a long time before coming up for air.

Killian was felt like a million bucks. He had just graduated college. He was at his parent's home and was swimming and had stayed under longer than usual. This time when he broke the surface, his head started hurting. It felt like someone hit him with a hammer. The pain was horrible. He could barely pull himself from the pool. He started vomiting. His pain was so bad.

He laid back on the ground and shut his eyes. Memories started flooding his mind, memories of his brother Arrow and his foster sisters Emma, Sage, and Skye. He remembered the boat and everything about that day. It dawned on him that his parents, who he loved more than anything, had been lying to him. My God, his brother Arrow and his sisters must have hunted everywhere in that lake for him. *What should I do?* He didn't want his parents to get in trouble. Killian knew he could never contact his brother Arrow because his parents would go to prison.

He confronted his parents. "You stole me. I wasn't your son. What happened to him. Did he die?" His father had a heart attack. "Dad, please don't die. I'm sorry I said anything. I will never tell a soul about what happened. Please don't die." Killian did everything to save his Dad, but he couldn't save him. His father died, not ever knowing how sorry Killian was for confronting him. He blamed himself. Killian shouldn't have told them. He knew they lied to him. Now he was the only one his mom had. All these years, he believed everything they told him, and it was a lie. Killian knew they loved him. He loved them too much to cause his mom any more heartache.

Killian joined the service and became a Navy Seal. Whenever

he got a chance to see his brother and sisters, he would go to Los Angeles, sneak around, and watch them. He was so proud of them. They made something of themselves. He met the woman he married on one of those visits. Mary Jo was beautiful and kind, and he loved her. What was really strange is she looked just like Sage Brooks, his foster sister. Killian told her when they met, she looked like Sage. She told him she was Sage's sister from another mother, and she couldn't tell Sage anything. She had to keep it a secret. Killian was tired of keeping secrets, but there wasn't anything he could do.

When his son was born, he named him Arrow Killian after him and his brother. They celebrated their fourth wedding anniversary when Mary Jo got sick. His son turned six months old when Mary Jo died of cancer. It almost destroyed Killian, but he had his son to think of. As much as he wanted to drink himself to sleep every night, he knew he couldn't do that. He always felt it wasn't fair that his life would go on without Mary Jo.

He was out on a mission way out in the sea in a miniature one-man submarine when it started falling apart. Killian woke up on a deserted island. He was there for a year before someone found him on that damn island. When Killian walked off the plane, his entire family was there waiting for him. He couldn't believe it, his brother and sisters, his son, and his Mom. How did they find him? They were all there together. The only one missing was Mary Jo.

KILLIAN

AUTHOR
SUSIE MCIVER

1

Killian Cooper couldn't believe that he was with his brother, Arrow, and his foster sisters Sage, Emma, and Skye. Before they found him, he hadn't talked to any of them for over twenty years. Arrow was laughing at something ex-Navy Seal Ash Beckham told him. His brother was marrying the woman he loved, Special Agent Brinley Ryan. Killian knew Arrow and Brinley loved each other more than anything. He lived a block away from them and always noticed how they looked at each other and held each other.

They stood, waiting for the bride. He watched as Brinley's friend walked out the back door. Killian's body turned hot every time he saw that woman. The first time he saw her he wanted her. He was hard before she took two steps. Her body could make a saint want to sin. She was beautiful. Out of the corner of his eye, he saw Brinley's two massive dogs, Lucy and Ethel, running in circles. He didn't blame them. Brinley made them wear dresses. A German Shepard and a Doberman Pincher. They were guard dogs, and she put pink dresses on them.

He watched as the hot-looking maid of honor tried to calm the dogs down. Then she let out a loud whistle, and both dogs ran at her. Killian watched as she tumbled to the ground. Her dress strap snapped off, and her dress hiked up around her hips. Killian chuckled. Those beautiful breasts of hers were about to fall out of her dress. She was wearing pink bikini panties. He took his jacket off, then picked her up, brushed her dress off, and kissed her. *Why the fuck did I do that.* "Sit," Killian demanded, looking at the dogs, who both sat down like they were angels instead of the enormous beasts they were. He straightened Bird's dress out again and buttoned the top of his jacket after putting it on her. He wanted her more than he has ever wanted a woman. His body betrayed him. He inhaled her beautiful scent. When his gaze met hers, he knew she wanted him to. This was crazy. Nothing like this had ever happened to Killian. Hell, this is the first time I've stood this close to her.

Arrow stepped forward. "Killian, let me introduce you to Bird Brewer. Do you remember your old Navy Seal buddy Jonah? He's sitting right over there. Bird is his sister and Brinley's best friend. I think she can stand on her own now."

Killian forgot he was still holding her. He didn't know what the hell came over him. Killian hasn't wanted to take a woman to bed since his wife, Mary Jo, died of cancer three years ago. Of course, that doesn't mean he hasn't taken one to bed. He was, after all a man, with strong urges. When he looked back at Bird, she was staring at him like she was in shock. "I'm so sorry. I don't know what came over me. Please forgive me."

"Don't worry about it," Bird told the tall, handsome guy whom she knew was Arrow's brother. She took a step towards him, and Arrow cleared his throat. *Was I going to kiss him? Yes, I think I was.* Brinley smiled.

"Shall we get back to the wedding?" Liam Price asked,

looking at both of them. Liam married Emma Stone, Arrow and Killian's foster sister. He was a pastor.

Killian walked Bird back to her spot, and he went back to his. He had never had this overpowering wanting feeling for a woman in his life. That made him feel guilty because of Mary Jo, but it didn't matter. He pushed the guilty feelings down. He knew she would be his for at least tonight. He looked at the dogs. "Stay."

Killian watched as his brother married his beautiful bride. He looked around at his family. They found him on that damn deserted island that had been his home for a year. He looked at his mom. She loved every one of his family members. They welcomed her into their family before they even knew if he was alive or dead. Why was he worried? They would never have had her arrested. Maybe Emma might have wanted to lock her up, but that was because he knew how much Emma loved him. All of his sisters were FBI Special Agents.

"Speech from the maid of honor," Emma called out.

Bird stood up. "I didn't know I had to make a speech. But here goes nothing."

"Say whatever you want to, honey. I'm sure it will be perfect," Killian said, smiling at Bird.

"Well, I met Brinley differently than most people meet someone. But I knew right away Brinley would always be my friend. She is so sweet and has such a kind heart. I had to call Arrow when I found Brinley with two bullet holes in her. She was out cold because someone hit her in the head with a piece of wood. Lucy and Ethel were only a little better off than Brinley. But look at them today, the happiest day of Brinley's life. She told me that earlier. I'm so happy for them," Bird looked at Brinley and smiled. If you looked in her eyes, you would see the laughter in Bird's eyes. "She even offered me her guardhouse for the night. Since I'm not leaving until tomorrow. That's how kind she is."

Killian grinned at her when she walked past him. He knew where he would be tonight. He thought back on his life. The time he spent on that deserted island with no one around for over a year.

Lieutenant Brice Allen, Navy Seal. Brice wasn't his real name; his parents told him his name was Brice. They falsified papers claiming that was his name. His actual name was Killian Cooper. He was half American Indian. He was in a boating accident with some other orphans and couldn't remember anything. His brother and sisters thought he had died that day. He looked up everything he could about the accident. He read where the police were always chasing the kids away from the lake, who were there hunting for their brother. There was a picture of Sage doing her famous high kick right in the guard's face. Six years ago, his memory came back. He remembered all of them. Arrow, Sage, Emma, and Skye. His family.

His brother and Brinley were the reason he was found on that deserted island. When his memory came back, Killian would go to Southern California and watch them. Killian would have talked to them, but he could never get over the fear that they would arrest his mom for taking him. He shook off all of his sad memories.

"Killian, it's your turn," Emma said.

Killian stood up and walked to where Bird had just left. She was still wearing his jacket. He figured he would pick it up tonight when he visited her at the guardhouse. Killian didn't know what he felt for Bird besides wanting her. "I'm so thankful to be here with all of my family, to stand up with my brother when he married the woman he loves, which is an honor I never thought I would ever have," he said. He looked around at everyone. Mary Rose held his son Kelly sleeping in her arms. Anthony sat next to them. They were Mary Jo's brother and sister. Killian wondered for a moment if they knew how much he wanted to make love to Bird. Then he looked into Bird's eyes and didn't care if they knew.

"Anyway, I thank God for Brinley finding me on that little island I called home for a year. I thank God for giving my family back to me," he continued. He walked over and took his son out of Mary Rose's arms. She had held him the entire time the wedding was going on. It was time he gave her back her freedom; Mary Rose was only twenty-nine. She needed to find a love of her own. Killian bent and kissed her. "Thank you for keeping my son safe."

Mary Rose wiped away a tear. "You are so welcome."

Killian held his son and walked over, and sat next to his mom, who cried. He put his arm around her. "It's okay, Mom. I'm going to be right here with my family always," he assured her. Killian still thought of Lillian Allen as his mother, even though she took him from the accident. She found him on the bank of the lake. She had just lost her son, and grief made her and his father not think straight. They knew he was an orphan, and that was all they thought about.

The party broke up at ten; with all the little ones falling asleep, Killian walked home with his Mom and Kelly his son. It was a beautiful night. The stars were out, and the moon was full. He put his son in the bed. "Mom, I'll be back later. I'm going back to Brinley's."

"Okay, dear, I'll see you in the morning."

2

Killian couldn't believe what he was doing. He was on his way to visit Jonah's sister, Bird, for one night. He walked around for a while, changing his mind about seeing her. Then he would picture her in his mind. He felt guilty for wanting another woman. This always happened when he was with a woman since his wife died. He didn't even know what the hell to do. He turned around and headed back home three times before he took a deep breath and walked back to the guardhouse. He knocked, and it was opened. Bird stood there looking beautiful.

"Hi," Killian said as he stepped inside. He pulled her into his arms and kissed her. Killian didn't give her time to change her mind. He felt bad about not asking her first. He raised his head and looked at Bird. She was beautiful. Her eyes were half-closed, and she wanted him as much as he wanted her. Killian saw it in the look she gave him. Her long blond hair fell down her back. Her beautiful eyes looked into his. "Say it right now if you want me to leave."

"No, I don't want you to leave. I want you to make love to me and do everything you want to do to me. And I'm going to do everything I want to do to you. Things I've never done before. We are going to make hot passionate love with each other all night long, then I go back home."

She raised her arms, and Killian pulled her nightshirt up over her head. That beautiful body of hers was his for the rest of the night, Killian picked her up, and she wrapped her legs around him. He put his hand between them, so he could feel her. She purred like a cat. That sound was all it took for Killian to lay her on the bed. He moved his hand, and she moved her body.

"Take your clothes off Killian, I want you to feel what I'm feeling," she whispered. First, his shirt came off, then his tee-shirt. He sat on the bed and took off his dress shoes and the rest of his clothes. He reached over and pulled Bird to him. As his mouth touched hers, he knew this would be something he had never felt before. When the kiss deepened, he raised his head and gazed into her eyes. He kissed her neck and down to her breast. His hands trailed down her body. His mouth followed everywhere his hands went. When his tongue touched her, she went wild. Killian could barely hold back. "Bird, I'm going to enter you now."

"Yes, Killian, please do."

It was the first time a woman had ever called him Killian. Mary Jo knew him as Brice Allen. Killian looked down at her as he was on the verge of entering her. She was so damn sexy. She was tight and hot. Killian made sure he satisfied her before he let himself release inside her. That was the first time of many times that night. He hoped she took a contraceptive. He had nothing in his wallet. He couldn't believe he didn't bring some condoms. They made love in so many ways. It was four in the morning, and Killian knew he had to get back to his son. He didn't want to leave. "Bird, I have to go in case Kelly wakes up."

"I know. I didn't expect you to stay all night," she sighed. Bird got up and went to the bathroom.

Killian walked up behind her. "Bird, I would stay if I could."

Bird turned in his arms. "I know. Killian, this was the best night of my life. I'm sure the things we did for each other will embarrass me later on, but I only feel wonderful at this moment. Thank you for tonight."

"Bird, thank you for tonight. It was more than I can ever say," he blushed. Killian felt guilt trying to take over, but he pushed it down and pulled her back into his arms. "Let's make one more memory."

Bird giggled, then she purred as his hand made its way down between her thighs. "Want to shower together?"

"Yes, it'll be a first for me," he admitted. They stayed in until the water turned ice-cold. Bird didn't want Killian to leave. How could she fall in love with him this soon? *No, I'm not in love with Killian. It was just an unforgettable night.*

Killian put his shirt on. He felt like he was in slow motion; he didn't want to leave. Killian held her wrapped in his arms for just a little longer. He bent his head and kissed her for another five minutes before leaving. "Bird, can I call you?"

"Yes," Bird wiped a tear off her cheek. "Bye, Killian."

Killian kissed her one more time before letting himself out of the guardhouse. He walked home with a lot on his mind. He didn't want to leave Bird tonight. Was it because it'd been a few years since he'd cared about who he made love with, and she was amazing? Killian knew he had to leave for California early, so he knew he had to sleep a couple of hours. He would think more about Bird tomorrow. At least he would be busy. Skye was going to take Kelly back home with her to California. Killian was relieved that he didn't have to worry about where Kelly would be.

~

KILLIAN RETIRED from the Navy and went into business with his Navy Seal buddies. They ran a high-security bodyguard and rescue team from all over the world. Killian mainly worked in the States because of his son, but he was still busy. He was guarding a country singer who had her life threatened at gunpoint. Killian and Ash would watch over her until they caught the guy. The crazy guy terrified her. The guy pulled his gun on her while she walked down the sidewalk. If someone hadn't come to her rescue, she would be dead. He took Kelly with him if he was going to be away for any length of time. He would take his mom with them, and she watched Kelly. Or they would stay at the safe house. They just got back from Los Angeles, and his son Kelly stayed with Skye at her ranch. He loved it there. It was full of orphans and animals. It made Killian remember how it was without his parents. He thought about adopting a couple of kids when his life slowed down.

It'd been three and a half months since he'd been with Bird, and all he did was think of her. He almost went to visit her, but he knew it must be the great sex that kept her in his memory. He didn't even know her. He asked Brinley about her, and Brinley said Bird stayed busy. She had her own large animal veterinary hospital. He dropped Kelly off with his mom and walked to Arrow's house, a block away. He buzzed the guardhouse and announced his name.

"Prove it."

"Excuse me?"

"I said, prove you are who you say you are."

Killian laughed. "Screw you, Ryker. Open the gate."

He walked through the gate. "Why are you here?"

"Because someone tried breaking our code here. People want Brinley. She knows everything about the government's computers. It's her code, and no one can crack the codes. But they still try. Arrow is madder than hell. You might not want to go around him right now. Brinley is still out of town. He's angry over that as well. I have an extra man coming in tonight to guard the house. What are you doing here? Arrow told me you were at Skye's. I love that place. Did you see Dakota while you were there?"

"Yeah, she stays away if I have anyone with me. Ash and I stayed at Skye's last night. I think Dakota stayed at your place."

"I gave her permission to stay there any time she wanted. She has her own room there. What are you doing now?"

"The guy who was after the singer got caught, so we were no longer needed. It feels good to be back home for a while. I'll see you around," Killian said as he raised his hand and walked up to the house. He walked down the long drive. There were dogwood trees on both sides. He felt like he had a second chance with his brother. Now they were neighbors. He could hear Arrow on the phone, and he didn't sound happy.

"You've been gone for almost two weeks, sweetheart. I miss you. What do you mean she's missing? Have you checked everywhere? You know Bird, she'll go out in the swamp and fix a toothache on an alligator. Honey, I'm not being a smartass. I know it worries you. I'll see you in a few hours. I'm going to call the airport right now."

"Was that Brinley?" Killian asked.

Arrow turned at the sound of his brother's voice. He had a frown between his eyes, thinking about Bird. It worried him that Bird hadn't answered her phone, but he didn't want to upset Brinley. "Yes, I'm going to go to her. She's upset because she says Bird is missing."

Killian froze. "What do you mean when you say she's missing?"

"Brinley went to Bird's pet hospital, and none of her workers have seen her in seven days."

"Maybe she went out of town?"

"If she did, she didn't tell anyone."

"Fuck, I'm coming with you. Let me pack a few things."

"Why are you going with me?"

"I'm going to find Bird. Why is no one watching over her? What does Brinley think happened to her?"

Arrow stared at his brother. "Why are you going to find her? You only met her once. The FBI is searching for her, and Brinley is calling Jonah. I'm sure they wouldn't expect you to go."

"Screw whoever, I don't give a damn what anyone expects. I'm going.

What case is Brinley working on?"

"There is a serial killer, killing blondes."

"Fuck, I don't give a damn what anyone expects. I'm going."

3

Killian and Arrow ran into Jonah and the rest of his Seal buddies at the airport. "Are all of you finished with your cases?"

"Yeah, Brinley called and said Bird is missing. I'm sure it's a mistake. Bird could be anywhere," Jonah said with a worried look on his face.

"Yeah, she called me too. The FBI is searching for her. Remember when she saved Brinley's life? She made a lot of friends with the FBI," Arrow said, walking into step with Killian, who didn't want to stand around talking.

"I'm going to check her house out first," Jonah said, looking at Killian. "What brings you along, Lieutenant?"

"Bird's missing. I don't need any other reason than that. I thought we were going to use our first names? I'm no longer your Lieutenant."

"We are. I'm sorry, sometimes it slips out. You were our lieutenant for years. I'll try to remember to call you Killian from now on."

"Jonah, do you think your sister is missing? Or do you think she went on a call and lost her phone?"

"I don't know. Brinley seems to think the serial killer has her. Bird usually tells her employees where she'll be. So they'll know where to look for her if the boat breaks down. She has a terrible habit of going off into the swamp on her own. I've tried talking to her about that. But she is so stubborn. One of her employees said her boat hasn't been moved."

"Why don't you have someone watching over her?"

Jonah laughed. "Did you hear me say she was stubborn? Bird does what she wants to do. I hope to hell she is at someone's house in the swamp. And that fucking killer doesn't have her. Of course, Bird won't sit idle and let someone take her without a fight."

"Does Bird know how to fight?"

"If the guy has her, she'll fight like crazy to get away from him. She can't fight like Brinley or your sisters, but she can kick and scream like in a girl fight. Brinley said there were six missing girls. The one they found last week had a note on her naming the girls who were with her. Bird wasn't on that list.

"Killian didn't say a word. He kept walking. Where is Bird's house?"

"Close to mine."

"We'll go to the pet hospital first thing in the morning. Arrow, where are you staying?"

"I'll be at the hotel with Brinley. Are you getting a room there?"

"No, I'll stay at Bird's house."

No one said anything. Jonah, Ash Beckham, Storm Anderson, and Austin Sawyer were used to how Killian gave orders. Jonah smiled, as did the other men. They missed their lieutenant shouting orders at them.

"Sorry, guys. Does anyone have another plan?" he asked. No one said anything. "Jonah, do you still have those boats you were always talking about?"

"Yes, they're even bigger and better now."

"Do you think we'll have to find her by boat?"

"I don't know. I need to talk to my grandmother to see what she says. She may have heard something."

As soon as they stepped outside, the heat hit them in the face. Even though it was dark out, it was still hot. The Mosquitos were buzzing their heads.

"Do you think your grandma is awake? If she is, I want to talk to her."

"I'll call her," he replied. Jonah got his phone out and dialed his grandma's number. She picked up on the first ring. "Grandma, it's Jonah. I want to talk to you about Bird. I have some of my buddies with me. Would it be alright if we came over?"

"I'll have sweet tea ready for you. I need to talk to you as well."

"We'll be there in thirty minutes," Jonah replied, then he hung up. "Okay, guys, grandma is waiting for us."

Arrow looked at his brother. "I'm going to go to Brinley. Call me if you hear anything?"

They walked over to the car rental. Killian rented a large vehicle. He wanted to get around on his own while he was here. Killian let Jonah drive since he didn't know where the hell he was going. *Where the hell are you, Bird?*

It seemed to take forever to get to grandma's; there were cars everywhere. "Fuck," Jonah cursed, hitting the steering wheel, "it's voodoo people. I hate being around these people," Jonah said, shaking his head. "Look, I'm going to warn you about something. Don't comment on their beliefs. You'll only piss them off. It must be pretty bad if everyone is here. Mention nothing about curses either. Or they'll put a curse on you. It must be pretty bad if everyone is here."

When he opened the screen door, everyone stopped talking. "Grandma," he picked an elderly woman up who had all kinds of things hanging around her neck. She kissed Jonah, then looked at his friends.

"Put me down and introduce me to your friends," she told him. Grandma looked at Killian and took his hand before Jonah said anything. She was about the height of her granddaughter, and her hair was still blonde. She wore it in a long braid down her back. When she looked at Killian, her sad smile reminded him of Bird. "Killian."

"Yes."

"I've heard about you. Bird told me you were lost on a deserted island for over a year. I am glad they found you. I won't tell you what else she told me."

"Thank you, I think," he replied with a smile. Killian wondered how she knew which one he was and then thought she must know about his Indian blood. Killian couldn't help but think it was some spiritual feeling she knew who he was.

Killian looked at all the people sitting around the living room with all kinds of stuff hanging from them. He was sure there were some alligator teeth. Some had decorated dolls sewed onto their clothes. "Look, I'm just going to come right out and ask this to all of you. Do you know where the hell Bird is? How is it she became missing? And why the hell was no one looking out for her."

Everyone started talking at once. Jonah looked at him and shook his head. Maybe he should have let Jonah do the talking. But Killian wasn't one to stand around when something desperate as this was going on. He didn't stop to wonder why he was here, but since he was, he would get to the bottom of Bird's disappearance.

He stood there with his arms crossed, waiting for someone to answer him. He knew the guys wouldn't say anything until someone answered him.

Grandma looked at him a minute before she spoke,

waiting to see if anyone had any objections to her talking to him. When no one said anything, she sighed and shook her head. She wiped the tears from her eyes, "We don't know where Bird is. But we spoke to Marc Breaux."

Killian looked around at the mention of Marc's name. He expected to see Marc walk in at any second before looking back at Grandma to hear what she was saying. He didn't realize Marc lived in this area.

"Marc said Brinley thinks the murders have something to do with someone taking a family member to a voodoo doctor to have their eyesight repaired. Because of the way he is killing the girls. He is torturing them and taking out their eyes. Marc's sister Mandy is missing as well. I don't think he's handling it too well. He's a mess. His parents died last year, three months apart."

"So, are you saying the killer went to a voodoo doctor?" Killian asked.

"We believe he must have gone to someone who does bad voodoo, and they told him what would fix the problem. When that didn't happen, which we know could not happen, he started killing. We know nothing for sure. We need to investigate more."

"Do you know any of these voodoo doctors who practice bad medicine?"

"Unfortunately, we do. We are meeting with some tomorrow."

Killian looked around. "Where will the meeting be?"

"At the FBI headquarters."

"Then, I'll see you there. Can you tell me where Marc Breaux lives?"

"Do you know Marc?"

"Yes, he was a Navy Seal with us. He retired from the Seals last year, so he could take care of his sister."

They said their goodbyes and then left.

Killian let Jonah drive. "Have you seen Marc since you've been out of the service?" Killian asked Jonah.

"I've seen him a couple of times, he was engaged to Edith," he shrugged his shoulders. "So I didn't see much of him. Edith didn't get along with many of our friends. I heard from Bird that they split up. I guess he finally opened his eyes to the real Edith. It's horrible about Mandy being missing. She's probably seventeen now. We have to find this guy. I just can't picture Bird letting anyone kidnap her. You have to know, Bird, she is very street-savvy. If she knows someone is taking girls, then she will make sure he won't get her. *Unless she thought she could save the girls.* He didn't say that out loud. "I always thought she and Marc would get together. Marc used to talk about her all the time in high school."

Killian didn't want to think of Marc and Bird together. He liked Marc and figured he would make someone a good husband, but not Bird. They pulled in front of a large home. He saw the outside lights come on, and Marc stepped outside. His hair was longer than it used to be.

"What the fuck! I thought you died in an ocean somewhere. Damn, it's good to see you," Marc said as he pulled Killian in for a hug. "What are you doing here?"

"We're here to find Bird, and now I hear we will also be hunting for Mandy. I'm sorry she's missing."

"Yeah, it's driving me crazy. She is so young. So you think Bird is also missing and didn't just take off somewhere?"

"Hell, if I know. Brinley seems to think someone took her."

"You know the hot FBI agent?"

"Brinley is my sister-in-law. Tell me, when did Mandy disappear?"

"Three weeks ago. I'm freaking out. I don't know if Mandy can fight her way out of a tight spot. She's more a nerd than a fighter. I'm afraid she won't know how to get away if she has a chance."

Killian knew his friend was shaking in his boots, worried about his sister. He couldn't stop pacing. "You need to take a deep breath and stop pacing. Have you eaten anything?"

"Brinley gave me a sandwich and soda earlier. I haven't been able to eat much, not knowing if Mandy's eating."

"I'll pick you up in the morning, and you can work with us while we're here. Can you call your work and take some time off?"

"I've already done that."

"While we are here, we'll help you find Mandy."

Marc sat down and bowed his head. It was like someone had lifted an enormous

weight from his shoulders. He felt hope come into his chest. His Seal buddies were here, and they would help him find his little sister. "Thank you, guys. You don't know what this means to me. I feel like I can hope; I haven't felt that before."

"We are helping each other," Jonah said, slapping Marc on the back.

Jonah dropped Killian off at Bird's and promised to pick him up at six in the morning. Killian walked through Bird's home. It surprised him at how large it was. He counted five bedrooms. Each room had a different theme. One was from the fifties, one from the seventies, and every bedroom had it's own era. She decorated the rest of her home with traditional furniture. All he could think was it fit Bird perfectly. He didn't even know Bird, so why was he thinking he did. He had one night with her, a night he thought of all the damn time. He walked into her room and looked at all the crystal figurines she had on her dresser. Her room was the twenties it felt as if you were in that era. *I'll stay here tonight.* He walked into the master bath, pulling his shirt over his head, ready to get into the shower. A note stuck on her mirror got his attention. He pulled it off and started reading.

"I'm going to kill her!" Killian shouted at the mirror. He reread the message.

Hi, Jonah, I'm guessing you are trying to find me if you've read this note. I have a plan. I'm going to let the killer catch me. I'm hoping he finds me soon. I've been walking around at night, waiting for the idiot to take me. I just hope it's the right guy who steals me. I'd hate for another weirdo to grab me. I have a plan to rescue the girls. Once I'm in there, wherever it is. I'll finish the rest of my plan since I don't know what I will find until I get there. Wish me luck, brother dear. I love you, Birdine Brewer.

Killian got in the shower. He thought he would give Jonah time to get to his place before sharing the message with him. He could smell Bird's scent. It made him hard. How the hell a smell could make him hard was beyond his thoughts. He washed his hair and smiled. It was strawberry scented. He had a towel wrapped around his waist as he made his way to the kitchen to see if she had something to eat. He barely ducked his head and reached for whoever kicked out at him. Arrow stood in the kitchen doorway, his brows raised. Killian looked down at who he had a hold of. Brinley turned to look at him at the same time.

"You can put your towel back on now," Arrow said with a smirk on his face.

Killian bent and picked up the towel. "Why the hell did you try to kick me?"

"I couldn't see who was in here. I only could tell it was a man. What are you doing here?"

"I'm staying here until we find Bird. I told Arrow I'd be here. Bird left a note."

"What do you mean, she left a note?"

"What I mean is I'm going to wring her frigging neck," he snarled. Killian looked around on the counter. He carried the note into the kitchen with him. He picked it up and handed it to Brinley.

"Why the fuck would she do this? What the hell was she thinking? Can she even fight? How would she know even where to go for him to grab her?"

"I don't know, but I have to call Jonah and tell him what's happening. He's her brother, he needs to know what the hell she did."

Arrow looked over at his brother. "Umm, Killian, you can get dressed now."

Killian looked down at his towel. "Sorry, I'm so used to running around with nothing on. I'll be right back."

As Killian dressed, his phone rang. He looked at the number and when he answered, he spoke the same time Jonah did. "Your stupid sister baited herself so the killer would catch her."

"Bird wanted the man to catch her. Damn, her. I swear when I get my hands on her, I'll make her wish she would have listened to me growing up."

"What are you going to do?"

"There is nothing I can do tonight. I'll see you at five in the morning."

Killian hung up his phone and went back to the kitchen. Brinley made sandwiches. Killian had his eaten in a few bites.

"That's one thing I missed on the island, bread. I remember the bread one of the foster mom's made. It was fresh and hot with melted butter. For some reason, I couldn't stop thinking about that bread."

"I remember her. She had all those kids of her own. But she still wanted to take care of the orphans. We're off to bed. Get you some sleep, Killian. Morning comes fast. I'm surprised you could remember that woman."

"I remember everything from that time. That's why it didn't surprise me when Emma tore into me for not calling when I got my memory back."

Arrow laughed. "She always was one to speak her mind."

4

Bird realized this was one of her more stupid plans. She had seen no other girls, but she knew they had to be here somewhere. This was a large building. Why is Mr. Tuttle killing girls? She's known him her whole life. His wife used to sing in the church choir with her. Until she lost her eyesight. Bird knew it had something to do with her diabetes. She was such a lovely woman. Bird felt terrible that she lost her sight. Zack Tuttle was a large man in stature. Bird figured he must be six and a half feet tall. She looked at his large hands, murdering hands. She couldn't stop the tremor that went through her body. These poor innocent girls.

"Mr. Tuttle, why are you doing this? Where is Mrs. Tuttle? I don't understand why you would kill these girls. Please say something. You can't kill any more girls. I won't let you."

"I knew I shouldn't take you, Birdine. But there you were walking up and down the street like you were asking for the killer to grab you." He squinted his eyes and shook his head. "Birdine, is that what you were doing? Were you wanting me to take you? Did you think you could save all the girls? I've already killed too many to stop now. I went to a voodoo doctor, and she said I had to take the eyes of twenty blonde girls, and my Sadie would get her eyesight back."

"That's crazy, and you know it. Listen to yourself talking. You're not making sense. You are killing these wonderful innocent girls so Mrs. Tuttle can see again? I bet she doesn't know what you're doing. God, you have to stop this right now. Let me take the girls and leave. You can't kill another one. I won't let you. Have you fed these girls? Do you bring them water?" she questioned. Bird was thinking about the small meager food he brought her every few days and a bottle of water that she had to make last a few days. "These damn mosquitoes are eating me alive. Can you bring me some spray the next time you come?"

"No, I can not. Why are you so worried about Mosquitoes when you're going to die. It's not your turn yet, but it will be soon. How are you going to stop me from killing these girls when you are now one of them? You're tied up Birdine, you can't get away from me. You've been trying for two weeks to break those bonds. Did you think I wouldn't see what you were doing, trying to untie those knots in your ropes? I'm the best in the state for tying knots. You and those girls have tried eating the ropes off your wrist," he scoffed. His laugh sounded like it belonged to someone else. It scared Bird. "My crab traps never came loose and floated away like a lot of peoples."

Bird didn't give a damn about crab traps. She knew she had to talk him out of killing another girl. She didn't know he even had this place this far back in the swamp. It was a large building. The small room he kept her in had no windows, and she had to use a bucket as a toilet. Bird looked around to see if she could see anything to let her know if the girls were here where she was. She saw the hooks and single cots made up for the alligator hunters who poached alligators out of season. "So this is where they take the poached alligators. Aren't you afraid someone will show up here to skin their poached alligator?"

"There won't be anyone coming here. FBI agent Rick Mills told everyone they can poach for free, as long as they tell him if they see a girl hanging upside down in a tree. So Bird, you've sacrificed yourself for nothing."

Why did I not notice his evil laugh before? He pushed her ahead of him, and Bird cried out as she fell on her knees. She couldn't stop herself. He tied her wrists and ankles. He untied her feet. "Get up," he said as he grabbed the rope and pulled. Bird cried out again. Her wrist was so raw from the tight rope. "Where are the girls? Stop this right now. What would your wife say if she knew you were doing this?"

"She would thank me. I'm doing this for Sadie, so she can get her eyesight back."

"I thought you were smarter than that. Why would you believe an evil witch? Did you give her money? How much did you give her?"

"Shut the hell up."

"So you gave her money. You can kiss her ass goodbye. I'm sure she's long gone, especially since you fucking did what she told you to do. What will happen to Sadie when they haul your ass off to prison? I'll tell you what will happen to her, she will be so disgraced, she'll die a slow death. The girls you killed were in her Sunday school class. Nope, you won't kill another girl. I won't let you," she raved. Bird might be petite, but she wasn't going down without a huge fight. She charged him as hard as she could, and he fell down. Bird ran to the other side of the room. She heard him laughing. She ran all around, trying to open the doors.

"I'm going to leave it up to you Birdine, Mandy is going to die tonight unless you want to take her place."

"No one is going to die. I told you, Zack Tuttle, I won't let you murder another girl," Bird cried. "It's stopping right now, do you hear me, you crazy bastard," Bird screamed.

"Get your ass over here," he pushed her out the door, and she fell again. This time he kicked her when she fell in the mud. Bird's body shook; she didn't want to die but most of all, she didn't want any more girls to die, but she wouldn't let him know it scared her. She read something once that killers love when they see how scared you are. They enjoyed seeing you cry and begging for your life. The swamp water was up to her calves, and she worried about the gators and the snakes, but more critical, she worried about the girls. There were so many flying insects. They were getting in her hair. Bird prayed there were no other girls murdered. She had to get them out of here. It was so dark, she couldn't see anything.

Then Bird saw a building ahead. *It must be where the other girls are.* Bird prayed to God that they were there.

"Get over here," he said as he pulled on her rope and twisted hard. Bird couldn't help the little cry that slipped through her lips. He unlocked the door and pushed her inside. This time, she was ready for him. Bird made sure she didn't fall down. It took a minute for her eyes to adjust, and it was still hard to see.

"Mandy, get over here. Your life is in Bird's hands. Either you die tonight, or Bird does."

"Bird!" Mandy cried and ran to her. Bird couldn't hug Mandy or any of the other girls who ran to her. He had all of their hands tied tight. Bird looked around; she couldn't see Sissy anywhere. Sissy lived down the street from Bird. She took care of her animals when she went out of town. She worked at Bird's pet hospital on weekends. "Where is Sissy?"

Pam started crying. "He killed Sissy, and he cut her eyes out and hung her upside down in the swamp. He said that's what he's going to do to all of us. So that Mrs. Tuttle can see again."

Bird couldn't breathe. He killed her. "She turned to the man and shouted as loud as she could. "You fucker! You are nothing but fucking slime. God is going to strike you down, you fucking bastard. Sissy never hurt a soul. You are a deranged mad son of a bitch. Girls go back over to the corner. This bastard isn't killing anyone."

"I'm the one who says what's going to happen here. Shut your mouth!"

"Fuck you!" Bird shouted. She saw the fist coming, and there wasn't anything she could do about it. Bird tried ducking her head, but he got her in the temple. She fell in a heap on the floor. The door slammed shut, but she didn't know it, she couldn't hear anything, she was knocked out. Five hours later she woke up. Bird didn't remember where she was for a second, then it all came back. She inhaled sharply and raised up. The girls were sleeping around her; Mandy was at her back. Bird turned over, and Mandy smiled at her.

"We have some planning to do," Bird whispered.

"Did you really get yourself grabbed on purpose? Mr. Tuttle shouted that after he locked the door."

"Don't call him mister, call him the bastard. He deserves nothing else. You can call him a fucker, but don't tell Marc I said that."

"Am I going to see Marc again?"

"Yes, we have many people hunting for us. When they find Sissy, they will triple the men and women. We are going to fight this bastard. He will get none of us.

Killian paced up and down in the front yard. He couldn't believe all the people hunting for this killer and the missing girls. He must have been on every inch of this swamp looking for them. *Bird, I swear when I find you, I will not let you out of my sight. What am I saying? I don't live anywhere around here. She doesn't belong to me, but I will find her.* Finally, he saw Jonah pull up. He looked at his watch; it was four in the morning. Damn, no wonder Jonah yelled at him for calling an hour ago.

"Do you sleep?"

"No, not until we find them, then I'll sleep. Today, I think we should go deeper into the swamp. I had a call from someone that said go deeper in the swamp."

"What! Who was it?"

"It was a woman's voice. Did they find the bad voodoo person?"

"They're close. I think my granny is putting curses on all the bad witches. I've always called them witches."

"Why do you think someone went to an evil woman who told someone to take the eyes of girls?"

"All the voodoo doctors have heard this. They're coming from all over to help. Word spreads fast in New Orleans. They'll have her name sometime today."

"Let's go see what we can find," Killian said, getting into the truck. "It's beautiful here. I wish it was for another reason I'm here."

"What's up with you and Bird?"

"We are friends. Can't men and women be friends?"

"You met her one day. She went back home the day after the wedding."

Killian shrugged his shoulders. "Friends, I don't let people hurt my friends."

"There's Marc. Is he going with us?"

"I don't know, I haven't talked to him this morning. He looks pissed off. He must have news."

"What's up?"

"They found the voodoo witch. She said the killer is Zack Tuttle. She told him if he could kill twenty girls with blonde hair and take their eyes out, his wife would get her sight back. They can't find him, but they believe he's with the girls. His wife, Sadie, is so shook up over this; she's not doing good. She had no idea he was doing this. A bunch of men took off already through the swamps."

"Who is this Zack Tuttle?"

"He's a church-going, man. His wife was a Sunday school teacher before she lost her sight. Tuttle is about six and a half feet tall. He's big gutted, and that makes him seem bigger. He has probably scared those girls to death. Pray to God he has killed no more girls."

It seemed to take forever going through the swamp. They followed the father of one girl. Killian saw the building and jumped out, kicked the door open, and stormed inside. He found the little room where one girl was held. Killian gave a loud roar and slugged the door, then he kicked it.

"Did that make you feel better?" Ash asked, looking into the room. "The motherfucker, this makes me sick."

"I'm going to kill him," Killian said, walking away.

"There is another building back there," he informed them. They walked behind the building and saw the shed. It didn't have windows. It must get so damn hot in there. Killian kicked the door open, and they heard the girls crying.

"Mandy!" Marc shouted. Mandy ran to him, crying hard. Tears ran down her face. Her hands were tied behind her back.

Pam's father stumbled into the shack. "Pammy, darling, are you in here?"

"Daddy, Daddy, I want to go home," she whimpered. He held her so tight, crying more than his daughter was.

"That fucker has her," Mandy told Marc, "Bird told me not to call him Mr. because he is a slimy bastard or a fucker. I will never repeat his name again."

"You call him whatever the hell you want to," Marc told his sister.

"Where's Bird?" Killian asked, looking at the girls.

"That fucker has her. Bird told him he would not kill another girl, and he slugged her. Then he came back and took her. He said she would have to sacrifice herself since she wouldn't let him kill one of us."

"When was this?"

"I think it was maybe thirty minutes ago."

"Fuck," Killian swore. Killian turned around. "Ash, you can come with Jonah and I. Marc, take your sister home."

The three Navy Seals marched back to the boat. Not one of them spoke. Jonah was going to the same spot they found Sissy. Twenty-five minutes later, they saw the boat. The giant of a man was dragging a kicking, screaming Bird from the boat. As soon as Killian was close enough, he jumped on the man. Jonah grabbed Bird and pulled her into the boat. She was fighting to go help, Killian. She watched as Tuttle picked up a large board and swung it at Killian, who ducked and kicked Tuttle in the gut. He went flying back and fell into the river. Before Killian could grab hold of the man, an alligator grabbed Tuttle, and then another one bit down on him. They were fighting over him, and then they took off with Tuttle. He was screaming like a man who knew death was upon him.

"Are you going to do anything?" Bird asked when Killian jumped into the boat.

"Do you mean before I wring your neck or after I wring your neck?" he asked. Killian looked at her. Her face was swollen from the hit she took from that bastard. Killian would have killed him again if he wasn't already dead.

"Why are you mad at me? All I wanted to do was help those girls," her lips trembled, and tears fell from her eyes. "He killed Sissy. Who would have never hurt a flea."

"I know. I'm sorry," he sighed. He pulled Bird into his arms and held her. Killian kissed the top of her head. You are so brave, Bird."

"No, I'm not. The entire time he had me, I prayed he wouldn't kill me. Can I go home and go to sleep now?"

"Yes, Jonah, let's take Bird to your house to sleep."

"You smell good."

Killian chuckled into Bird's hair. "It's your shampoo. I used it. It reminded me of you."

"Did you want to remember me?"

"I will never forget you," he vowed. Killian held on to Bird as Jonah made his way back to his place. He knew he had to leave. His son needed him. It wasn't up to his mom to watch Kelly for him.

Brinley waited on the bank of the river for them. "Bird, thank God, where is that bastard?"

"The alligators got him."

"Good, he deserves what he got. While you shower, I'll heat you some stew I made."

"Thank you, Brinley."

Brinley looked at Killian. "Are you going to let her go?"

Killian smiled. "Yeah, I'll let her go."

Bird looked at him and knew he was leaving. "Why are you here, Killian?"

"I'm here because a serial killer took someone I care about."

Bird sighed and kept on walking. She walked into her old

room, stripped out of her clothes, and put them in the garbage. She cried like a hungry baby wanting its bottle. Bird cried for Sissy and the girls who that fucking bastard murdered. Bird cried because Killian was leaving, and she would never see him again.

When Brinley opened the bedroom door, Bird was in bed sleeping. She tiptoed away from the room. "She's sleeping," Brinley said, walking into the kitchen.

"I need to be heading home," Killian said, looking at all of them. "I'm going to tell Bird, bye, whether she's sleeping or not," he declared. He walked back to the bedroom and looked at Bird. The white sheet made the bruises stand out more. He bent and softly kissed her lips. "Goodbye, Bird. I'll remember you always," he said. He took a small crystal bloodhound out of his pocket and set it on the nightstand where she would see it when she woke up. He found it in a shop downtown and knew she would love it.

HE WAS PICKING up his son when his phone rang. Killian didn't look at the phone number. He just answered. "Hello."

"Did you steal my shampoo?"

Killian took a deep breath. "I wanted something to remind me of you. When I start missing you, I take a shower and shampoo my hair."

BIRD CHUCKLED. "Do you miss me, Killian?"

"I'll always miss you, Bird."

"Then why did you leave? Come back."

"I have my son, and he needs to live around his family who love him. I could never take that from him."

"You're a great father, Killian. Thank you for the crystal. I love it. Goodbye."

"Bye, Bird," he breathed. He turned off his phone and did his best to put a smile on his face for his son.

He heard his son laughing as he walked up the front steps,

"You're back. Did you find Bird?" Mary Rose said as she opened the front door.

"Yeah, we found her. I swear to God, she makes me so mad. Can you believe she put herself in front of that damn killer so she could save those girls?"

"Did she save them?"

"Yeah, she saved them. We got to her just in time. He was dragging her away when we found her."

"Do you care for her, Killian?"

"Bird lives in Louisiana. I live in Washington, DC. I feel guilty for having feelings for her. It could never work for us if I feel guilty for being with her."

"You listen to me, Killian. Mary Jo has been gone for three years. She wouldn't want you feeling guilty. Find your happiness, Killian. You deserve to be happy. Go after Bird if that's who you want."

5

"Sadie, I don't mind you being here. You know I enjoy your company. I don't see why you have to go to your brother's home."

"Bird, you have your hands full, taking care of Grace and your job. You don't need to take care of me. Besides, I enjoy my brother's home. I can lie out on the deck and get a tan."

Bird chuckled. She went looking for Sadie Tuttle when no one had seen her in weeks. She found her in a rundown place on the wrong side of New Orleans. The woman who rented the room to her called the church and told them about Sadie. She said the woman stopped eating and was killing herself over the grief of the murdered girls.

When the pastor told Bird, she wasted no time going down there and taking Sadie Tuttle back to her place. That was eight months ago. She realized she was four months pregnant, not long before that. She gave birth to her daughter Grace. Bird always had a problem with her period not being on time, sometimes she would go months before having her period, so when she was late, she paid no attention. Bird barely gained any weight, and when she started gaining weight, she didn't tell anyone about the baby. Jonah was gone most of the time, working with Killian and hisNavy Seal buddies. Bird didn't want to worry him, so she never said anything. She would break out in a cold sweat when she thought of being near that killer while pregnant with Gracie. Gracie was the love of her life. She showered her with all the love she had in her. Grace was a happy baby. She made everyone who came into contact with her smile.

Bird made Jonah swear not to talk about her and the baby to anyone. She also made Marc swear it. She didn't want any man who didn't want her. Sure Killian wanted her, but you couldn't make a happy home out of sex, no matter how good it was. Killian didn't want her around. She would have moved to Washington if he had asked her.

Now here they were, standing in the Los Angeles airport waiting for the man to bring Sadie's suitcases. It didn't take long. Bird spotted him before he spotted them. She thanked him for his help when she felt someone looking at her. She turned her head, and Killian stood behind her. *Oh my God, what am I going to do?*

"I thought I heard a sexy southern voice. How have you been, Bird?"

Bird didn't say a thing for a minute, then she saw Kelly and Mary Rose walk up and stand next to Killian. *Are they together now?*

"Hello, Bird, how are you? It's been so long since I've seen you."

"Hello, Mary Rose, I'm doing wonderful, thank you. How are you?" she asked. Bird forgot how beautiful Mary Rose was.

"I've gone back to my law practice. So I'm busy, as you can imagine."

Bird looked down at Kelly, who had a hold of Mary Rose's hand. Hey there, Kelly, you're growing so fast.

"Hi, I'm going to be as big as my daddy."

Bird chuckled. "Yes, you are."

Killian watched her close. "What are you doing here in California, Bird?"

"I'm taking my friend to her brother's in Carlsbad. Why are you all in California? Did you move here?"

Killian looked at Bird and realized she thought he and Mary Rose were together. Before he could correct that assumption, her friend called out to her.

"Bird, I think Grace is hungry."

Killian watched as Bird dashed over and picked up a baby girl. Her hair was as blonde as her mama's. Bird laughed at her and kissed her face. Killian felt like someone punched him in the gut. He didn't want to think of another man making love with Bird.

"Whose baby is this?" Killian asked, even though he knew the answer. He had to hear it with his own ears.

Bird smiled down at the baby. "This is Gracie. She's my baby."

Killian held his breath. "How old is she?"

"She's three months. Gracie is big for her age."

"Can I see her?"

"I don't know, she doesn't like strangers," Bird replied with a frown on her face. He held his arms out and Bird reluctantly handed Gracie to her daddy, holding her breath. If he looked at her eyes, he would see his own looking back at him.

"Hello, Gracie. She's beautiful. She looks like her mother. Who's her father?"

"No one you know."

"I see Jonah all the time. He never mentioned you having a baby."

"I guess he doesn't enjoy talking about his unmarried sister having a child."

Killian acted like he didn't hear her. He would ask Jonah himself why he never mentioned the baby. "Who is this?" Killian said, looking at Sadie while still holding the baby.

Bird reached for her baby and introduced him to Sadie. "Killian, this is my good friend Sadie Tuttle. Sadie, this is Killian. Mary Rose, and Killian's son, Kelly, are standing next to him."

KILLIAN RAISED his eyebrows at Bird. She raised her chin a little higher. Sadie Tuttle. It was just like Bird to take care of someone whom the town probably turned against. He turned to Sadie as he handed the baby back to Bird. "It's a pleasure to meet you, Sadie. I hope you enjoy your visit with your brother."

"It's nice to meet all of you. Bird has told me so much about you. Sometimes I wish I was stranded on a deserted island. But now it will be better to live on the beach with my brother. He wants me to stay with him always. I'm blessed to have such a kind brother. But I'm going to miss Bird and Gracie so much."

"Well, I guess we'll be seeing you guys," Bird kept her head down. She didn't want Killian to see the tears pooling in her eyes. *Damn it, Bird, you better not cry in front of them.*

"Your baby is big for three months," Killian commented.

"Yes, I said she's a big baby. She's healthy, and she loves to eat," she added. All the time she talked, she kept her head down. "Goodbye, Killian. It was nice seeing all of you again, Mary Rose, goodbye Kelly. Maybe we'll bump into each other again sometime."

"You should come out to Skye's ranch. Everyone is going to be there. It's something about a surprise for Emma and Axel. Jonah will be there."

"I'm sorry, I need to be somewhere else this weekend. Thank you for inviting me."

"Who is Gracie's dad?"

"No one, you know," Bird answered again. She took Sadie's arm and pushed the stroller with the other hand. The man with the suitcases followed behind.

"Are you going to be all right?" Sadie asked, patting Bird's hand. She could feel her dear friend trembling.

"I will be in a minute."

"Is he Gracie's father?"

"Yes."

"Why didn't you tell him about Gracie? I knew when you said she was three months, he must be. She looks every bit of the six months that she is. I can tell that, and I'm blind."

Bird chuckled. "With those fat cheeks and her giggling, she looks nothing like a three-month-old. She's big for a six-month-old."

"Do you love him?"

"Yes, isn't that crazy? I've only spent one night with him."

"You should tell him."

"He's with someone else now."

"Mary Rose pushed Killian as he stood watching Bird walk away. "Go after her."

"It's too late, she found someone else."

6

"What the hell are you talking about? Hell no, Bird. I swear to God, you are not moving."

"Jonah, I'm twenty-eight. You can't tell me what to do anymore. Besides, you're in California more than you are here. You should sell your house. You don't have to come back just to visit Gracie and me anymore."

Jonah ran his fingers through his hair as he paced. What the hell is going on with you Bird? Why are you moving?"

"I want something else. Gracie needs me to be with her more. I'm missing the first months of her life working all the time. I want to have a veterinarian clinic next to my home so I'm with Gracie during the day."

"Why don't you just tell me who her daddy is?"

"Why would I do that? It doesn't matter who he is?"

"Does he know he has a daughter?"

"I don't want to talk about him. I called to tell you I've sold my veterinarian hospital and my house. I've packed all my belongings. I'm on the way to my new life."

"What the hell Bird, why didn't you call and talk to me first? Where are you moving to?"

"I don't know yet. When I find the town, I'll call you."

"What the fuck do you mean, you don't know? Damn it, Bird, you can't be driving all over the United States hunting for a town to move to with a baby. Is this about Tuttle and the murders? Damn it, Bird, wait until we can talk about this. You have Gracie to think about now."

"I am thinking about Gracie. That's why I'm moving. I don't want to live here anymore; it has too many bad memories. People won't stop talking about what happened. Sometimes I stay up all night because I'm scared someone will break into my house."

"Why didn't you tell me about this? Go to my house. I'll be there in a few hours."

"I'm a grown woman with a child. I have to take care of my own life. I'm already on the road. I've been on the road for a month now. I'll call you soon. I promise," she finished. Then she hung up and turned off her phone. "Okay, Gracie, we've been on vacation long enough? It's time we get serious and settle down. I miss my animals, and I'm sure they miss us."

Gracie slept as Bird drove. Grace was going to be one in a month, and Bird wanted to have her new home by then so she could throw her a birthday party. She pulled into a rest area and took out her map. *Which way do I want to go? I should have figured this out before now.* "Gracie, why don't we head to California? I went there in college, there are beautiful towns to live in. Let's move to a small town where nothing crazy happens. I'm ready for a quiet life. What about you?" Bird kept on talking as she drove her truck down the freeway. She had to get over this sadness that was hanging over her all the time. She decided she would drive six hours a day, then stop and rest for the night.

7

Killian looked at Jonah. "Did you talk to Ash? He has had no luck finding Katy Campbell. Do you have any ideas?"

"Hell no, I don't, I can't even keep up with Bird. She sold everything in Louisiana, and she and Gracie have hit the road. I've been trying to get a hold of her, but she shut her damn phone off. Bird doesn't even know where she wants to live. She said they are driving around the United States to see what town she likes. Isn't that fucking crazy?"

"What do you mean she's hit the road?"

"Bird doesn't know where she wants to move to. She hasn't decided on a town or State. She's been on the road for a month already."

"What about Gracie's father? Doesn't he have a say in anything?"

"Her father. I have seen no one around Bird except you. At first, I thought you were the father. You and Gracie have the same eyes. I don't know anyone else who she's been with."

"Gracie is seven months now. Why would you think it was me?"

"Gracie turns one in two weeks. Why did you think she was seven months?"

Killian added up the months and couldn't breathe. His body turned to mush. *My baby!* Why wouldn't she say something? She kept his baby from him, knowing he missed those early years with Kelly. "I'm going to kill her. Why didn't I see this? I held Gracie at the airport. Bird said she was three months old and was big for her age. Why wouldn't she tell me?"

"She told me Gracie's father was with someone else. Maybe she thought you were interested in someone. You've brought Mary Rose to California with you and Kelly every time I've seen you here. Maybe Bird heard something. She talks to Brinley. Maybe Brinley mentioned you and Mary Rose taking vacations together."

"We haven't taken vacations together. Mary Rose has come to California with Kelly and me a few times. There was nothing to it. Damn it, Bird," he roared. His fist banged against the table. "What am I going to do?"

"Hey, I can't even get her on the phone. She's turned it off. She'll call me soon though, it's Gracie's first birthday. Bird is big on birthdays. She'll call me and let me know where she lives or where she's moving to."

"Let me know when you find out. Fuck, I'm not waiting around for her to get in touch with you. I'm going after her. I don't know what I'm going to say, but that's my daughter, and I will be in her life. I promise you that."

BIRD SAW the girl on the freeway and wondered what she was doing out here with nothing around anywhere. *Should I or*

shouldn't I. I'm sure she's a runaway. Bird pulled over but kept her window rolled up. She saw the girl hesitate before coming close. Then Bird saw her. She knew who she was. Bird saw her on the news that morning. *Katy Campbell.* The reporter had said that strangers took her. Bird figured there must be something else going on. She looked scared to death. Bird rolled the window down.

"I'll give you a ride, but you better not try anything. I have a baby in the back seat. I'll throw open the door and push you out if you try anything."

"I won't try anything. I promise. Thank you so much for the ride. I was so scared. It gets cold at night up here. I've had to hide on the road from so many people."

"There are some chips and a soda in that ice chest right there. Help yourself. What are you doing out here with nothing around for miles?"

"I'm just exploring America."

"That's what Gracie and I are doing too. But I think I know the town I want to live in."

"Really, you're driving around hunting for a town to move to? Why? Are you running away?"

"I guess in a way, I am. I wanted to go in search of something new. We've been on the road for six weeks now. Gracie will be one tomorrow, and I don't even have a house yet to throw her a party. Everyone should have a birthday party. Don't you think so?"

"I'll come to her birthday party. If you have one tomorrow, I'll go to it. I can't buy a gift, I have no money. Thank you for the chips and soda. It's delicious."

"You're welcome. What's your name?"

"Katy."

"I'm Bird."

"Your parents named you Bird?"

"It's Birdine, but I go by Bird. Is Katy your nickname?"

"Yes, my name is Kathleen."

"Will your parents worry about you?"

"My mom died last month. It's only my stepfather. He's not a nice man."

"I'm sorry. Why don't you hang out with Gracie and me? We need to find a house. You can help me look. Have you ever been to Temecula?"

"No, Mom and I used to take long drives when she wanted to get away from Gene. That's my stepdad. My real dad lives in Spain. I remember him from when I was younger. But I haven't seen him in years."

"Do you ever talk to him?"

"Gene didn't allow Mom and me to call my dad."

"Why not?"

"He's horrible. He has a lot of money so he can make things happen. Mom feared him all the time. We ran away once; bad things happened to my mom when he found us. Katy wiped her eyes. My mom told me if anything ever happens to her, she wanted me to run away and hide from him."

"Are you scared of Gene?"

"Yes, he wants me to become his wife."

"He sounds like a real creep. Don't worry, you won't become his anything. I'm going to dye your hair when we get to a hotel," Bird offered. Bird looked over at Katy. "I have to admit I knew who you were. I saw your picture on the news. It said strangers took you."

"No, I wasn't taken by anyone. I left on my own."

"I'm going to tell people you're my sister until I can get you some help. I could use some help if you want to stay with me for a while. I'm sorry, I always jump in and try to take over people's lives."

Katy wiped her face with her shirt sleeve. "Bird, I'm so

happy you picked me up. I don't care if you take over. I didn't know what I would do."

"I'm happy I picked you up too, honey. You are going to have a new name. From now on, I will call you Lucy," Bird giggled. "My friend has two dogs, named Lucy and Ethel. Isn't that funny?"

"My mom and I used to watch *I Love Lucy* late at night. She would come into my room and watch TV with me."

"Do you know your dad's phone number in Spain?"

"No, I don't think he likes me."

"Why would you say that?"

"Because I never got letters from him. Gene never let Mom or me have a phone."

"The more I hear his name, the more I dislike him. Did you see that sign? It says we only have twenty miles to go. I'm going to stop at the drugstore and get the dye. What color hair do you want?"

"Can I have it blonde like you?"

"Yep, you sure can."

8

Jonah kept hearing his phone beep. He crawled out of bed and looked at the clock. It was four in the morning. On his phone were pictures of Gracie. She was so precious. She looked like Bird. She was laughing at something someone was saying. He laughed out loud at some photos of Bird and Gracie. Then another image popped up with Gracie and a girl. What the hell, who is that? She seems so familiar. He dialed Bird's phone number.

"Bird, it's been three months." Her brother shouted over the phone, "Where the hell are you?"

"Jonah, I miss you too. I had some things to take care of. I need your help."

"What kind of help?"

"Lawyer help. Can you come for a visit?"

"Of course, what the hell kind of trouble are you in?"

"Do you want my address, or do I need to call another lawyer?"

"Give me your address."

"I live in Temecula, California."

"You moved to California?"

"Yes, I just told you where I live. Do you want the address?"

"Yes, give it to me," he replied. Jonah wrote down the address with a big grin on his face.

"When can you get here?"

"In about twenty minutes."

"What! Where are you?"

"I'm in Temecula. I'm following a lead on someone," he answered. That's when he recognized who the girl reminded him of, Katy Campbell. Has Bird been hiding this girl from her father? He knocked on Ash's door, then he knocked on Killian's door. He dreaded being there at the same time as Killian when he first saw Bird and Gracie.

"What's up? Why are we waking up at four in the morning?" Killian asked.

"I got a call from Bird. Here are some photos of Gracie on her first birthday," he handed Killian his phone. Killian walked into the other room and looked at them.

Killian looked at the pictures of his baby girl. She was beautiful. Her smile was like her mommy's. Killian clicked to the next image. It was Bird and Gracie kissing. There were eight photos and then one of Gracie and a girl who looked so familiar. Crap, Katy Campbell.

He walked back to the other room. "Where is she?"

"She moved to California, Temecula, California. She's about twenty minutes from here."

"What! Did you say she moved to California? I moved to California. We both live in California. Let's go."

Killian couldn't believe Bird was this close, and he didn't feel her presence. He was a little nervous about seeing Bird and Gracie. "Why is Katy Campbell with Bird?"

Jonah shrugged his shoulders. "Let's ask her when we get there."

They pulled into a long driveway with weeping willows

lining both sides of the lane. Ash whistled as they spotted the house. "Wow, this is a nice place."

Killian spotted the veterinarian clinic behind her house. There were three horses in the meadow. Bird stood outside, drinking a cup of coffee. When she spotted Killian, she turned around and went back inside. He jumped out of the truck and followed her into the house. Ash and Jonah gave them some time together before going inside.

"Bird, stop right where you are. What the hell is going on with you? You have my baby and disappear. You lied to me about how old Gracie is. Why would you keep my baby from me?" he questioned. He watched her; she was more beautiful than ever. Her hair was loose, hanging down her back. She was dressed in jeans and boots and a blue top that matched her eyes.

Bird backed away from Killian until she came into contact with the counter. "You have your life, Killian, and Gracie and I, have our life. You told me you have your son, and I had no part in your life. I asked you to stay, but you didn't want me enough to ask me to go with you. So don't you even think to blame me for keeping Gracie from you. You moved on in your life, and I've moved on in mine."

"What the hell does that mean?"

"It means I don't need you in my life because I have your child. Don't think you can take Gracie from me either because you'll have one hell of a fight on your hands. I can guarantee that."

"Bird, I don't want to take Gracie from you, but I want her in my life. She's my daughter."

"You have Kelly and Mary Rose. I only have Grace."

"What the fuck do you mean I have Mary Rose? She's Kelly's aunt, and that's all she is. I'm not with any woman. I haven't been with any woman except you. Why would you think differently?"

"It has nothing to do with me who you date. I will let you visit Grace, but she's my baby. I won't let you take her from me."

"I don't want to take her from you. I swear talking to you makes me so confused. I thought you might care enough for me to tell me I have a daughter," he returned. Killian turned when Jonah and Ash walked inside. He watched as Jonah hugged his sister. He would give anything for one of those hugs. What's the matter with her? Why did she think he didn't want her?

Killian got down to business. "Why do you have Katy Campbell here? How the hell did you end up with her?"

"How do you know about Lucy?"

"Lucy, who the hell is Lucy?"

"I've changed her name so her step-dad can't find her. He's not a nice man. And I won't let him take her. Brinley found her real father. And he's on his way here. Gene Watson told Katy's father that she and her mother died in an accident years ago."

"What the fuck are you talking about? He's worried to death about her. He hired us months ago to find her and bring her back home. I can't believe you've been hiding her here all this time."

"He is not worried about me!" Katy shouted, looking at Killian. "He wants me to marry him. I'm not going back there."

"What are you talking about?"

"He's a cruel, evil man who has beaten both my mom and me. If he thought we were hiding something from him, he would go nuts. We tried running away, but he caught us. My mom died because he wanted me as his new wife. She told me to run as far away from him as I could if something happened to her. I'm never going back there. He tried to rape me. If someone hadn't shown up, he would have."

"Are you telling me he wants you to be his wife?" Killian demanded, frowning.

"Yes. I won't go back."

Killian looked at Bird. "How did she end up with you?"

"I picked her up when she was walking on the freeway a few months ago."

"You picked up a hitchhiker?" he roared loud enough to wake up Gracie.

"Now, look what you've done. I'll be right back. I have to get my baby."

"I already have her," Brinley said, walking into the room.

Killian turned toward Brinley, his sister-in-law, who held the most beautiful baby he'd ever seen. Gracie rubbed the sleep from her eyes and smiled when she saw all the people in the kitchen. He looked at Bird, who had a massive grin on her face.

Brinley looked at Bird. "Is she going to meet her daddy today?"

"Yes, hey there, sweetie, let me see you. I have a surprise for you," she said. She walked to Killian. "This is your daddy," she told Gracie. Bird handed Grace to her father and watched as her daughter stared at Killian. Then she gave him a huge grin and kissed him.

Killian thought he might cry right there in front of everyone when Gracie farted and giggled. He threw back his head and laughed. He loved this precious baby of his. "She takes after her uncle Arrow."

"I need to feed her breakfast," Bird said, holding her arms out for Gracie.

"I'll feed her while you and Katy tell Jonah and Ash about Gene."

Jonah held his arms out. "First, I'm going to hug my niece."

While Killian fed the baby and Katy talked to Ash and

Jonah, Bird started making a breakfast of bacon, fried potatoes, and fresh eggs from the many chickens she had running around the chicken coup. She was thankful for this property. When she got into town, she talked to a realtor who told her about this place. It hadn't even gone on the market.

Bird didn't waste time even looking at it. She bought it on the word of the realtor and a few photos. The vet that owned the place was retiring to Florida. Bird loved it the moment her eyes saw it. She even took over his clients.

She mixed up some of her mama's famous biscuits. She sliced some tomatoes and green onions, took out some Tabasco sauce, then put everything on the table with the food. "Breakfast is ready."

Bird watched as everyone filed into the kitchen and took a seat. Killian scooted Gracie close to his chair and filled his plate.

"You're going to love Bird's cooking," Brinley said, making herself a plate of fried potatoes gravy, biscuits, eggs, and bacon.

"Umm, this is so good, I miss your cooking, sis. I think I'll stick around for a while. I'm in California so often, I might sell my place and move to this town, near you and my niece.

Killian looked at Jonah. "You have that case in Michigan."

"Not until the first of the month. I'll bring my things from the hotel tonight."

Killian looked over at Bird. "I'll pick up Kelly from Skye's and be back tomorrow. Ash can stay here until I get back. Keep Katy inside. I don't know who else he's hired to find her. Someone knows she's here. They tipped us off that she was in Temecula," he said. Killian turned his head. "Do you know who tipped us off?" he asked Jonah.

. . .

"Austin got the call. Hang on," Jonah took his phone out of his pocket and left the table. Moments later, he was back. "He said it was a message left because the guy didn't want anyone to know who he was," Jonah said, setting back down to finish breakfast.

"So it could have been anyone. I think I'm going to pick Kelly up and come back tonight. We'll stay awhile, so we can get to know my daughter."

Bird couldn't believe Killian would think he could just move in with her. He didn't even ask her he just took it for granted because she had his baby.

"What are you talking about? This is my house. You can't just move in here. Don't you remember telling me you couldn't take Kelly away from Mary Rose and the rest of his family? I don't want you here. It's hard enough having you sit at my table, let alone having you here overnight. Having Gracie doesn't give you the right to stay here."

Killian knew why Bird didn't want him here. They both knew it was because they would end up in bed together. Nothing had changed with them wanting to make love to each other. That was another reason he didn't want to have Jonah there with them. "I'll help with the dishes, then I'll be on my way," he said. He saw her sigh in relief. He smiled. "We'll be back before bedtime," Killian told her. Killian turned to look at Brinley. "Are you staying another night?"

"No, Arrow said I've been gone long enough."

"Does Arrow know Gracie is mine?"

"Killian, look at her eyes. Anyone could see she's your baby. She has your eyes, but Arrow doesn't know. He's never seen, Gracie."

He would have liked it if Brinley was staying another night with Bird. In case he didn't make it back before dark.

Bird started clearing the table. Then she looked at him.

"Do you want to dress Gracie for me? I need to finish up and get to work."

"Do you work in the building behind your house?"

"Yes, my vet clinic is behind the house. I usually take Gracie with me. And Katy helps me out with her, as well. I loved having Katy with me. I'm going to hate to see her go."

"Why don't I take Gracie with me?"

"Are you crazy? Grace doesn't even know you. No, you are not taking her with you. Damn, how did it get to this?"

"Okay, don't get upset, I'm sorry. It was only a suggestion. I'll dress Gracie for you. Where is her room?"

"Katy, will you please show Killian to Gracie's room?"

KILLIAN LOOKED around at Gracie's room. It was a room any little girl would want. He set her in her crib and picked her something warm to wear. Everything was so cute, he didn't know what to put on her. He decided on some little pink leggings and a cute dress to go over it with some soft shoes. Then he put a sweater on her and kissed her. "Daddy loves you and your mama."

"Why don't you tell her, mama?" Brinley said, walking into the room.

"She doesn't like me much right now."

"Killian, you know Bird, she isn't like us. Her feelings get hurt easily. When I asked her why she hadn't told you about Gracie, she said, you have enough people in your life. When you told her you had to stay close to Kelly's family, she thought you meant Mary Rose. Because I got to tell you, Killian, Arrow, and I both thought the two of you had something going on. I mean, what man takes a woman with him every time he goes out of town if nothing is going on?"

"I didn't take her with me every time," Killian stopped to

think. "Maybe I took her with me a lot. But we have nothing going on. She's Mary Jo's sister. I want her to know she will always be a part of Kelly's life."

"What about Anthony? Do you always invite him? He's Mary Jo's brother."

Killian thought for a moment. "I wonder if everyone thinks something is going on between Mary Rose and me."

"Well, I can answer that question for you. The answer is yes, all of your family thinks something is going on between you two. In fact, they are wondering when you'll pop the question."

"What! All of them think I'm going to pop the question? I wonder what Mary Rose thinks?"

"You'll have to ask her that question. How come you didn't ask Bird to come with you after the murders? You left, then Jonah left. Bird was scared someone was going to kill her. She never slept. Did you call her after the murders to check up on her? Is it any wonder she said nothing to you about Gracie? Bird is my friend. You have lots of people in your life. Bird doesn't have many. If you screw with her, I'll make sure you pay. I don't care if you are Arrow's brother."

Killian looked at his beautiful sister-in-law. With her long black hair and those beautiful eyes. He knew Brinley could kill you in a second. She wouldn't kill him, but she could make him feel like crap. Killian walked out and around the back where Bird fed the horses. "Bird."

"Yeah," she said, dumping a bag of oats into a feeder. She smiled when she saw her daughter. "Look how pretty Daddy made you," she kissed her on the neck, and Gracie grabbed her hair and giggled. Bird laughed and pulled her tiny finger out of her hair. "Did you want to ask me something?"

"Did you think Mary Rose and I are dating?"

"Are you two still together, or did you break up?"

"We've never been together."

"It's none of my business who you want to date. Can you please put Gracie in her playpen? Katy is inside, answering the phones for me."

"Bird, will you please look at me?"

Bird raised her face up to his, and gave a deep sigh, and turned around. "What is it, Killian?"

"I want you to know nothing is going on between me and any woman. How could I ever want another woman after being with you?"

"You've got to be kidding, right? I'm sorry, Killian, I have to feed the animals. I don't have time to listen to your nonsense."

"It's not nonsense. If I didn't think you were with someone else, I would have already been with you."

"So it's my fault."

"I didn't say that. Why don't you let me take Grace with me? I'll be careful, I promise."

"Killian, she doesn't know you. She'll become scared when she can't see me.

Killian, how do you expect me to take you seriously when you haven't tried seeing me in over a year? We've seen each other one time since you came to Louisiana. And that was by chance. You never called me or tried to see me. How can you say you care for me?"

"I thought you found someone else when I saw the baby. I thought you were with another man."

"But you didn't know that because you never tried to see me or call me. Now can I please get back to work?"

"Because I thought you and Gracie's father were together. Damn it, listen to me. I would have been there if I knew you weren't with someone," he tried to explain. Killian knew he was wasting his breath talking about this right now. She climbed over the fence and walked toward the horses. "I'll be back by dark."

9

Ash heard someone outside the clinic, and it didn't sound right. He looked at Bird and walked close to her. "Take Gracie and Katy in the back and lock the door."

"Why?"

"Someone is outside."

"It's probably Jonah. He said he would be right back."

"He wouldn't be sneaking around. Go now."

Bird grabbed up Gracie and took hold of Katy's hand. "Someone is outside. I want you to take Gracie and hide in that secret room I showed you. Don't come out here until I come and get you. I'm counting on you to keep Gracie safe if these are bad guys."

"Come with us. I don't want anyone to happen to you."

"I can't leave Ash out there alone. What if they are bad men?"

"If they are working for Gene, then you can bet they are bad people. I'm scared to leave you out here."

"I know, honey. I'll be fine. Please go before it's too late," Bird said and turned to her daughter. "Gracie, sweetheart, mama loves you so much. Katy is going to keep you safe," she kissed her and handed her over to Katy.

Katy ran to the door that led into the house. She hugged Gracie, picked up her diaper bag with everything inside, and went to the secret room in the house's walls. No one would ever know this room was here. Bird kept it full of water and snacks. It even had a small bathroom.

Bird went back to the front of her office. She spotted Ash outside, looking around on the grounds. "Oh, crap," Bird spotted the man hiding behind the bush by the window of the shed. She knew she had to do something. As she watched, another man came around the horse corral. He had a gun. She had to warn Ash. Bird ran around the room, hunting for a weapon. She saw the man aim his gun at Ash. She picked up the horseshoe from her counter and opened the door. She threw the horseshoe at the man with the gun, and it hit him in the back of his head. He turned and fired his gun before he fell to the ground. Ash turned around in time to see Bird fall to the ground.

"Fuck!" he shouted as loud as he could. He ran to Bird, calling for an ambulance at the same time. "Bird, please be okay."

"There's another man behind the bushes," Bird whispered as Ash bent over her. "Ash, the secret room."

"What secret room?"

"Gracie, secret room."

"Don't move. I'll be right back. The police are on the way."

Bird didn't hear him. She couldn't hear anything. She didn't hear her brother when he pulled up into the yard, shouting when he saw his sister lying in a pool of blood. She didn't know Ash had to kill a man or that he was going crazy hunting for Gracie and Katy. Bird didn't hear the police when they pulled into the driveway with their sirens blaring.

"Bird, where is Gracie?" Ash asked over and over even

though she couldn't hear him. He looked at Jonah. "I'm going to call Killian. Where the hell could Gracie and Katy be? They have to be here somewhere," he growled. The police wanted a statement, and the EMTs were working on Bird.

Jonah raised his head and wiped a hand over his face as a tear streamed down his cheek. "Did she say anything before she blacked out?"

Ash thought back. "Yes, she said secret room."

"Secret room. Maybe there is a secret room in the house."

"Then why the hell didn't she get in it? I told her to hide."

Killian's phone wouldn't stop ringing. "I just got out of Temecula. What's up?"

"Killian, you need to come back."

"Why?"

"Bird's been shot. I can't find Gracie and Katy, and the police are here. I killed a man who tried killing me. The EMTs are working on Bird. I kept her alive until they got here."

Killian turned around and stepped on the gas. "Who the fuck shot Bird?"

"There were two men. I told Bird to take Katy and Gracie and hide, but Bird thought I needed help. She saw a man with a gun sneaking up on me. Bird threw a horseshoe at him. It hit him in the head, but before he blacked out, he shot her. I killed the other guy. The police have the shooter."

"How is Bird?"

"The ambulance just left for the hospital. I don't know. The bullet hit her in the chest. I can't find Gracie or Katy."

"I'll be there in twenty minutes. They have to be hiding, and Katy is too scared to come out; she might think her stepdad is there." *Damn, I should have stayed there. God, please don't let Bird die. Where the hell should I go?* "Listen, Ash, you can find Gracie and Katy. I'm going to the hospital. I need to see how Bird is doing. If you have to take those walls apart, then do it. They have to be there."

Killian pulled into the parking lot of the hospital and saw Jonah pacing on the sidewalk. He didn't even notice Killian walk up to him. "Jonah, how is she?"

"She's going to be fine. The doctor is taking out the bullet. It hit nothing major. She woke up while we were on our way here."

"Did she say where Katy and Gracie are hiding?"

"She wouldn't tell me. She says she wants to make sure Gene Campbell is behind bars first."

"Maybe that's a good thing. We'll make sure he's arrested. I'll kill the bastard if I get my hands on him. If he sent men to Bird's house with orders to kill, then he's a sicker bastard than we thought. I'll find out where they are, I'm sure she will tell me. I'm Gracie's dad."

"You can try to ask her. You know how stubborn Bird can be. If she thinks someone will hurt Katy or Gracie, she won't say a word."

"Bird knows she can trust us to keep them safe."

Killian didn't like the hospital. The smells brought back so many memories of Mary Jo. He practically lived at the hospital when she was going through all those cancer treatments. He tried blocking out all of those memories. It did no good to remember sad times.

They were sitting in the waiting room when the doctor came in. Both men stood up.

"Are both of you here for Birdine Brewer?"

"Yes, how is Bird doing?" Killian asked before Jonah could speak.

. . .

"SHE'S GOING to be as good as new. She will only have a small scar. She can go home in a couple of days, as long as she takes it easy. She's a lucky woman. The bullet missed her organs."

"Thank you. She'll take it easy if I have to tie her down."

"You can visit her when she's moved to a room. She's already awake, but I don't think you want to see her before she calms down. She wants to go home right now. She seems to think if she's home, everyone will be safe."

"Yes, my sister thinks she can do anything."

Killian looked at Jonah. "Let me go in first. If she's going to fight with me, I would rather not have an audience."

Jonah laughed. "You better than me."

Killian walked into Bird's room, and Déjà vu hit him in the face. He hurried to her side and took her hand in his. He bent his head and kissed her. "Damn it, Bird, do I need to glue you to my side to keep you safe?"

"I'm not going to argue with you. I'm so thankful you're here. Keep Katy and Gracie safe. I'm going to tell you where they are. You can't let anything happen to them."

"Nothing is going to happen to anyone. I'll keep all of you safe. Where are they hidden?"

"They're in my secret room. It's behind the kitchen door. When you shut the door, feel with your hand, the middle of the wall. Push it, and it will pop open. Don't let any strangers on the property."

"SWEETHEART, no one is going to hurt Katy or Gracie. I'll kill the person who tries to hurt them."

"Killian, I didn't mean to get shot, but that man was sneaking up on Ash. What was I supposed to do?"

"You saved his life. You are always saving someone. That's what kind of person you are. That's one of the reasons I love you."

"You love me? Killian, you don't have to tell me you love me. I don't think you even know what love is."

"What do you mean, I don't have to tell you? I know what love is. Bird, I love you. Because of you, I know the power love can have on a body. I've loved you since that night we were together. You just need to accept it because I'm not taking it back. So you're going to have to live with it."

"Okay, whatever you say. Now, will you go keep our daughter safe until I get home?"

"Yes," he took her face in his hands. "I should have told you that night. I hate to admit I felt guilty that night. Because I've never had that powerful feeling come over me before. Nothing like that has ever happened to me. I thought it was a betrayal to Mary Jo. I wanted it to last forever. I didn't want to leave you that night. But it wasn't just the night. I didn't want to leave you ever. When I heard you were missing, my heart stopped beating. I knew I had to find you even if I couldn't have you. I always knew where you were, and I needed you to be safe. I know you don't want to hear this. I've known from the beginning you weren't interested in an always. But I'm not keeping it to myself anymore. I love you!"

A tear slipped out of the corner of Bird's eye, and he wiped it away. "Killian, I'm sorry, but I don't think you know what genuine love is. Our daughter is over a year old, and you never came to see me. You never called me. You went on with your life without me. How can you say you have loved me since that night? You never tried to see me after that night. If you loved me, nothing would have stood in your way. Not even the guilt you said you felt. You felt something for me that you didn't feel for Mary Jo. I don't know what it was besides great sex."

He opened his mouth to deny what she was saying, but Bird held up her hand. "I don't want to talk about it anymore," Bird asserted. She shut her eyes until he left, and then more tears fell. He finally said what she wanted to hear, but it was a year and a half too late. Bird would not let his pretty words turn her head.

Killian was still mulling over what Bird said when he pulled into her driveway. He noticed another car and remembered Katy's real dad was supposed to be there. When he turned his truck off, Ash and another man walked up to him.

"How's Bird?" Ash asked right away. "She saved my life."

"She's going to be fine. The doctor said she could come home tomorrow."

"This is Katy's father, Stephen. He's come to pick his daughter up."

"No one is taking Katy anywhere until Bird's home. She almost died because Katy's stepdad wants her," he declared and looked at Katy's father. "Do you know why he wants her? Because he wants to marry your daughter. I'll bet you anything. He killed her mother. The more I find out about him, the more I want to make sure he's locked up for a very long time."

"Do you know where my daughter is?" Stephen Morris asked.

"She's hiding on the property somewhere to keep her and Gracie safe. You two look in the barn. Jonah and I will look over here."

"We've looked everywhere," Ash said.

"Keep looking," Killian said as he walked to the house.

As soon as Killian walked into the kitchen, he shut the door and felt the wall. It snapped open. He smiled, wondering why anyone would need a secret room. "Katy, it's Gracie's dad. You can come out now, honey. Bird told me about the room. Your real father is here too."

"Where is Bird?"

"She's at the hospital. Don't worry, she'll be home tomorrow," he assured her. He spotted Gracie playing on the floor and picked her up. "Let's shut this up so no one can see Bird's secret room."

"Why is Bird in the hospital? I heard the siren. Did she get hurt?"

"Yes, but she's going to be okay. Ash caught those two men. I'm sure your step-dad is under arrest right now. I'll make sure he's locked up. You can stop worrying. Are you ready to meet your father?"

"Will you stay with me?"

"Of course. Have you eaten anything?"

"Yeah, there is always food in the secret room."

Killian chuckled. "It's just like Bird to find a place with a secret room."

When they walked outside, Ash and Stephen walked around the house. Father and daughter looked at each other, and Katy cried. "Daddy!" Katy said as she ran to him.

"Baby," he hugged her to him. "I'm sorry I believed him when he said you and your mom had died. Can you forgive me?"

"Daddy, he killed Mama. He gave her poison. I know he did."

"What? Do you truly think he killed your mom?"

"Yes, Mama thought so too. She said she was getting sicker every day. She told me he scared her and that she wanted me to leave. She hid some money for me, but Gene had already gotten it when I went to get it. Daddy, are you going to leave me?"

"Never, I will never leave you, baby, I promise. I have always loved you. I will always love you. You're my daughter, and where I go, you go."

Killian was sleeping in the same room as Gracie. He wouldn't let her out of his sight. The love he felt for his baby girl shook him. He was sick of the way he treated Bird. Who the hell did he think he was? Bird was right. He didn't know what real love was. He thought his passion for Mary Jo was the most profound love there was. But he was wrong. The love he felt for Bird was true love. It was so intense his heart ached. Killian loved his wife, but that was a sweet love. What he felt for Bird Brewer scared him. If Killian would admit it to himself, that was why he didn't go to her. He feared losing her. The love she had in his heart was scary.

He lay there next to his baby girl and let the tears fall. Killian knew he had to fix this. Killian had to make Bird realize how much he loved her. He would spend the rest of his life trying to show her whether or not she wanted him to. He had to say goodbye to Mary Jo and put the love he had for her aside. He and Kelly had a new life now with Bird and Gracie.

10

Bird was a little sore, mostly when she bent over. She cuddled Gracie to her. At least she would always have Gracie. She already missed Katy, who went with her father to Spain. They were exhuming Katy's mother's body so they could see if Gene had poisoned her. Killian told her Gene Campbell will stay behind bars. The money he had now belonged to Katy since her mother had the money to start with.

Jonah went back to Louisiana to sell his home, and Killian was still in Temecula. Bird went about her business as if nothing happened. She had always lived by the saying, "Live for today tomorrow might not come." So that's what she had always tried to do. But sometimes, it was damn hard.

KILLIAN COULDN'T FIGURE Bird out. It'd been a week since she got out of the hospital, and she acted as if nothing happened. He was leaving today to get Kelly and bring him back here. He needed to find a place close to Bird's house. He had to go because he had a new case, and it was his turn to watch over someone. They tried taking turns sitting with whoever they were guarding. It wasn't fair for one guy to have to watch over someone who had their life threatened. He was protecting a very wealthy woman whose ex-husband wanted her dead. He had a photo of her and recognized her right away. She was with the FBI right now. Julia Sparrow was bringing her to their place in Los Angeles. When they realized most of their jobs came from California, they bought a few safe houses in that State. Killian had no idea there was so much money in this business. It afforded him with enough money to buy a home anywhere he wanted to live.

He watched Bird as she went about her business as if she had never been shot. "Look at your mommy working away. Let's go see if I can take you to Skye's so we can get your brother."

"Bird, when will the colt be due?"

"In about a week. This colt will be big," she sighed, "I need to advertise for some help. I'm busier here than I was in Louisiana. I never realized how many cowboys and cowgirls lived in California," she admitted. Bird turned and looked at him and Gracie. "Are you getting ready to leave?"

"Yes, I need to get Kelly. I wanted to see if Gracie could go with me?"

"Killian, you know I hate to let her go anywhere," she replied. Bird would like to go with him anytime she wanted. She wished he were hers to keep. She could kiss him whenever she wanted to. He was trying hard to show her he loved her. Bird knew that, but he didn't come around her until he learned about Gracie. She had to remember that. If it wasn't for Gracie, she would have never seen him again.

"What are your plans, Killian?"

"I plan to bring my son here so he can meet his sister. I'm looking around for a place. I have a realtor helping me look. I have a case that I need to be in Los Angeles for in a few days. Julia is bringing someone to our place in L.A. for us to guard. So until I can get my own place, I wanted to let Kelly get to know Gracie."

"Are you saying you want to take her for the entire night?"

"Yes."

Bird knew he would watch Gracie. He loved Gracie almost as much as she did.

"Okay, please be careful with her. She's all I have."

"Bird, sweetheart, she is not all you have. You have me. I love you. You do know that, don't you, Bird?"

"I know if it wasn't for Gracie, I never would have seen you again."

"Why do you say that? You didn't have Gracie when I went to Louisiana. I came here because I love you. That's the reason I'm here. I love Gracie, but you are the only reason I'm here."

"I'll pack Grace some things. I'm going to miss her."

"We'll see you tomorrow."

He raised her chin and kissed her. He pulled her into his arms. "I love you."

KILLIAN PULLED into Skye's yard in the afternoon. Most of them were in the yard. He went to the backseat of the pickup and took out Gracie.

"Oh, Killian, she's beautiful. She has your eyes. How old is she?"

"She's fifteen months. Gracie, meet your Aunt Skye."

"Skye, this is Grace, but we call her Gracie."

"Gracie, what a beautiful name. I'm surprised Bird let her out of her sight."

"She almost didn't. Where is Lucas?"

"He's on a case. Gunrunners, I think. Of course, he won't tell me. Are you staying the night?"

"Yes, I wanted Kelly to meet his sister, and then I have to be in L.A."

"How's Bird doing?"

"You know Bird, you wouldn't even know she had been shot if she didn't squint in pain once in a while."

"How's it going with you two?"

"It's not going well with us. Bird says I don't know what love is. She thinks because I never went to be with her before I knew about Gracie, then I must not love her like I claim I do."

"What do you think?"

"I think I didn't go because I felt so guilty for loving her with so much passion. And I felt like I was betraying Mary Jo's love."

"Fuck, I hope you didn't tell her that."

"Why?"

"Well, it makes you sound like a pussy, and it sounds like a stupid excuse."

"I told her that. Crap. I don't know what to do."

"Killian, do what you did on the night Gracie was conceived. It must have been pretty spectacular."

"It was everything. Okay, that's what I'll do. I will not take soft footsteps around her anymore. When I tell a woman I love her, I mean what I say. Do you have anything to eat? Gracie and I are starving. Where's Kelly?"

"He's playing games upstairs. Go get him. I'll take Gracie. Come back down to the kitchen. I'll heat some leftover chicken."

. . .

Killian leaned against the door and watched his son play and laugh with the other kids. He spotted his dad and ran and jumped in his arms. "I missed you, Kelly."

"I missed you too, Daddy. Are we going to get Mary Rose now?"

Killian realized he screwed up putting Mary Rose in Kelly's life so much. "We live in California now. Mary Rose lives in Washington, DC. We will visit her when we can. But she doesn't live with us. I have a surprise for you."

"You do. Is it a toy?"

"No."

"Is it candy?"

"No."

"What is it?"

"Let's go down to the kitchen, and I will show you."

Kelly tried guessing all the way downstairs what his present was. They were almost at the kitchen, and Killian turned toward his son. "Close your eyes. No peeking."

"I'm not."

They stood in front of Gracie, Killian picked her up. "Open your eyes."

Kelly looked all around. "Where is my present?"

"Right here silly, you have a baby sister."

"My present is a baby?"

"She's your sister. Don't you like her?"

"Does she pee on you?"

Skye and Killian busted out laughing. "Not if she has a diaper on."

"Then don't take her diaper off. I don't like baby's pee."

"I thought you would love your baby sister. I almost had to sign my life over to get to bring her with me."

"Can I go play now?"

"Don't you want to know her name?"

"I know her name. It's Gracie. Uncle Arrow told me about her. It's okay, Dad, I like her."

"I'm taking him with me tomorrow. He'll never want to leave here if I don't. I'll figure something out when I get back to Bird's tomorrow."

"You know you can always leave him here."

"I know. Thank you!"

"Are we almost there?" Kelly asked him for the tenth time.

"Yes, we are almost there. Are you eager to see Bird again?"

"Is she going to be my new mom?"

Wow, where did that come from? Killian wondered. His son was so smart for five. "Would you like Bird to be your new mom?"

"I don't know. Does she like boys?"

"She loves boys."

"I thought Mary Rose was going to be my mom."

"Mary Rose is your aunt."

"Okay, are we going to live with Gracie?"

"We'll talk about this another time. When I know the answer," Killian mumbled to himself.

Bird was with the horses when Killian pulled up with the kids. She walked to him. He was lifting Kelly down.

"Hi, Kelly, wow, you've grown so much."

"I'm going to be big like my daddy."

"Yes, you are," Bird leaned around Killian to see Gracie, who had a massive smile on her face. "Hi there, baby girl," she smiled. Gracie held her arms out, and Bird picked her up, giving her hugs and kisses, making Gracie laugh. Bird turned to Kelly. "I bet she loves her big brother."

"Yes, she likes it when I make faces at her."

"Do you know what big brothers do?"

"Yes, they take care of their little sister."

"Wow, you're not only growing. You are also smart."

"I'm really smart."

"Yes, you are. Why don't we go have lunch, then you can feed the chickens for me?"

"I'm a good chicken feeder. I feed Aunt Skye's chickens."

"That's wonderful," she remarked. They were walking to the house with Killian following, carrying their suitcases.

Killian couldn't have been happier as he listened to Bird and his son talking like they were old friends. He didn't know why he was nervous about them getting along. Everyone loved Bird. They spent lunchtime laughing with Kelly and Gracie.

"I'm going to put Gracie down for her nap, then we can feed the animals."

"Okay," Kelly said, yawning.

"I'll tell you what, why don't we feed the chickens now, and Killian can put Gracie down for her nap. When we finish, you can rest a bit before your sister wakes up."

THE REST of the week flew by. Killian and Kelly helped Bird with the animals and played with Gracie. When it was time for them to leave, Bird didn't want them to go. She knew she was going to miss them. They had just put the kids to bed. "If Kelly wants to stay here with me, instead of going to Skye's, he's more than welcome."

"Are you sure?"

"Yes, I'm sure. I enjoy having him here with us. Besides, if you love me, that might mean we will be a family one day, right? So he and I can get to know each other better."

Killian pulled her to her feet and wrapped his arms around her. "Does this mean you believe I love you?"

"Yes, I know you love me. I never doubted that. My doubts were how much you love me. I want my husband to love me more than any other woman. I don't want someone who feels guilty for wanting me. I don't want my husband to put me second, behind his wife who died."

He took her by the hand and walked with her to her room. There he undressed her, all the while taking his clothes off too. "I don't feel guilty anymore. I love you with a different love than I had for Mary Jo. The love I feel for you is so powerful and passionate. It takes my breath away. It makes me ache thinking of you. I love you so much. It's all I can think about."

"This will only be the second time we've made love," Bird said with a catch in her voice, "I hope I remember everything."

Killian chuckled. "It'll all come back. It's the second night, not the second time. We made love dozens of times the first night."

Bird was breathless. His touch scorched her skin. She touched him as much as he touched her. Bird felt him shiver at her touch, and that gave her the confidence she needed.

She pulled him onto the bed, his lips trailed kisses all over her face. With each kiss, he told her how much he loved her. Tears were on her face, and Killian kissed them away. She loved him so much, she knew she should tell him, but she didn't say a word. They made love until three in the morning when both of them fell asleep in each other's arms.

Kelly woke them the following day. Bird hid her face and pulled the covers to her chin. Killian chuckled when Kelly commented Bird had forgotten her pajamas. "Gracie and I are hungry."

"Go tell Gracie we'll be right there. Don't take her from the crib, though," Killian said.

"Okay, but I'm big enough to."

"I know, but don't."

"I won't. Are you awake, Bird?"

"Yes, sweetie, I am."

"Good, you cook better than my dad."

"As soon as you go into the other room, we'll get up," he told his son. Killian watched as he ran out of the room. He swatted Bird on the butt. "Come on, sweetheart, if I have to get up, so do you," he pulled the covers back and looked at her.

"You look beautiful this morning."

"You look handsome this morning. It makes me want to stay in bed with you all day. I'm almost ready to have an orgasm just thinking about you."

"Hey, that's not fair. You can't say things like that and leave me wanting more."

"What time are you leaving?"

"This afternoon."

"Then I'll meet you back here when the kids take their nap."

"It's a date," Killian said, bending down to kiss her. He couldn't stop his hand from finding her under the covers. She moaned into his mouth.

Killian was telling the kids goodbye when he turned to Bird. She had just wiped a tear from her eyes. He didn't want to leave, but this was his business too, so he had to pitch in. They were becoming popular, and everyone wanted to hire them. He decided to look up more of his Seal buddies and see if they wanted to join them.

He held her in his arms and kissed her as he held Gracie in one arm, and Kelly had a hold of his leg.

"I don't want to leave you. You know that, right?"

"Yes, I know that. I don't want you to leave, but I know you have to go. I promise I won't get into any trouble while you are gone."

"I love you, sweetheart."

"I love her too," Kelly piped up.

Bird chuckled as she ruffled his hair. "I love you too."

"Who me?" Killian asked.

Bird hoped she didn't live to regret her following words. "I love both of you."

He looked into her eyes and kissed her again before handing Gracie over to her. "I'll see you in a week. If not, I'll call and let you know."

"Okay, drive carefully."

11

Killian looked at the woman whose life he guarded. She was the most stubborn woman besides Bird he'd ever known. Her ex-father-in-law put out a hit on her because his son ran his car off a cliff when he was drunk. Since Avery Talbot divorced the stupid man's son after three months of marriage. He blamed Avery, even though they were divorced two years ago.

"Avery, I've told you it doesn't matter if he's in jail. The hit is still there. Stay inside until we catch whoever is trying to kill you."

"I've been inside for five weeks. Don't you have to go see Bird and your kids?"

Killian smiled. She was always trying to get under his skin. He should have never told her about Bird and the kids. She enjoyed telling him he was missing out on family stuff.

Avery Talbot was a top private investigator. The man she married was cheating on her right after the wedding. Being an investigator, she investigated him. And had photos she showed him. Then she divorced him. He was a drunk who died in a fiery crash, and his father blamed Avery for his death. Killian liked her. She reminded him of Emma Stone, his sister. When she opened her mouth, swear words came out.

"It will not work, so you might as well stop right now. I left Bird a message this morning. They know I have to stay here with you until they catch the killer."

"Maybe he's changed his mind."

"He's already been paid. He is a professional, and he'll do his job until it's done. That job is killing you. After he does that, then he'll stop."

She turned and went into the other room. Killian wished to hell they would catch this bastard so he could go back to Bird. He had just stepped out onto the back deck when a bullet hit him in the leg.

"Ash, get her. He's here," he said. Ash got Avery and made her get on the floor. He watched as another bullet hit Killian.

Killian laid on the deck. He couldn't move. He knew that if he did, the shooter would shoot him again. He saw Ash arguing with Avery. He didn't know what it was about, but he could bet she wanted her gun. He wondered where Storm was. Then he saw movement out of the corner of his eye. It was Storm hiding in the damn tree. How did he get there? God, I hope he's not spotted, or he won't have a chance. Killian felt himself floating; he didn't have any pain. It was like someone gave him something to put him asleep. He wondered for a brief moment if he was dying. He thought of Bird, Kelly, and Gracie. He prayed to God not to let him die.

AVERY WATCHED as Killian drifted in and out of consciousness. There was a lot of blood on the ground. She saw the lock in the door turning and knew one of the others was back, and the door was wide open to the shooter. She crawled like a snake to the door. "Don't come in unless you're on your stomach. There's a shooter, and the door is wide open to him."

The door opened, Jonah was on his stomach.

"Who are you?"

"I'm Jonah Brewer. What the fuck is going on?"

"There's a shooter, didn't you hear me the first time? Or maybe you have to have everything repeated to you?"

Jonah ignored her. He crawled over by the French doors and saw his lieutenant and best friend on the deck in a pool of blood. He had to reach him.

"Don't try it. He will shoot you too."

"Why the fuck are you right here. Shouldn't you be in one of the other rooms? Maybe under the bed. Why are you in this room?"

"Because I'm going to kill that bastard. I need a gun. Killian took mine from me."

Jonah looked at Avery Talbot. "Stay the hell down. I'm going to get Killian. Call for an ambulance."

"An ambulance, are you crazy? That man will kill those ambulance drivers. You have to kill him first."

"Where are Storm and Ash?"

"Storm is in the tree. Ash told me to stay here and stay down. . I think he's going to try to sneak up behind the guy."

"Fuck, I have to get Killian. My sister will never forgive me if he dies."

"Are you Bird's brother?"

"Yeah. Do you know my sister?"

"I know about her. Killian's told me about her and the kids."

"Oh," he said shocked. That surprised Jonah that Killian

would mention his private life with a client. She must have weaseled it out of him.

A shot rang out, and they heard a thud. Jonah looked out the back and saw Storm on the ground. "Fuck!"

That's when the doorbell rang. "Why is everyone picking today to visit?" Avery muttered to herself. "If you know what's good for you, you'll leave as fast as you can. There is a shooter in the back, and he's already shot two people."

"Open this fucking door," a woman's voice bellowed.

"Okay, but you need to get on the ground. Because the door is in the path of the shooter," she notified the woman. Avery reached up and unlocked the door. And to her surprise, a blonde woman crawled inside. She didn't wait around for introductions. She made her way to where she could see the back deck.

"Killian, fuck, where are the other's?" Emma shouted.

"They're around here somewhere."

Emma frowned, looking at Avery. "I have to get my brother in here before he dies."

"Brother, who's your brother."

"Killian."

"Emma Stone, I presume."

"Yes," she replied. Emma got to the French doors when she spotted the guy getting braver. He was in the damn palm tree. What a stupid ass; when he turned to aim again at Killian because he saw Killian's leg move, Emma stood and aimed. The guy was dead before he knew what hit him. "Call an ambulance!" Emma shouted as she ran out the back door.

"Fuck, I swear to God, Killian, if you die, I will never forgive you."

"Shhh, don't get upset, Emma. If I don't make it, I have to ask you to watch over Bird and the kids."

"Shut the fuck up. Nothing is going to happen to you. But if it eases your mind, I promise I'll watch over them.

Now let me see your injuries. Hey, can you get me a pair of scissors?" Emma called over her shoulder. Jonah ran to Storm as Ash jumped over the back fence. He looked over at the shooter, who was dead. Emma's bullet hit him between his eyes.

"Stay alive, Killian, please stay alive!" Emma shouted at him.

"Here, let me see him," Avery said as she cut Killian's pant leg up to his hip.

"I was a nurse before I became a private investigator. This bullet went through. He got hit twice. Help me find..."

Before she finished talking, they saw where the blood was coming from. It was on his side. When they pulled his shirt up, blood came from a horrible-looking hole in his side. The bullet was still in there.

"This looks painful."

"It is painful," Killian said. He tried taking a deep breath, but it hurt too much.

"Emma, I have something I want to ask you."

"You want me to watch over Bird and the kids? I already said, I will. Killian, you are going to be okay, so please stop talking about dying."

Avery then went over to check Storm. He had a hole in his shoulder. The fall from the tree knocked him out. His head hit the fountain under the tree. When the ambulance arrived, they put Killian inside. Avery looked around. Then she looked at Jonah.

"Am I free to go?"

"No, not yet. We have to wait until Killian okays it."

"Why?"

"It's the way it goes."

Emma looked over at Avery. "Do you want to ride with me to the hospital?"

"Yes, thank you. By the way, I'm Avery Talbot.

"I kind of thought you might be. I'm going to call Bird. She's Jonah's sister. Killian is madly in love with her."

"I know he told me he was in love with Bird. I hope he pulls through this."

"He will. That's why I'm going to call Bird. She'll make sure he does."

12

"Here comes Bird," Emma said. She and Skye met Bird in the middle of the hallway. She was carrying Gracie, and her other hand had Kelly's little hand in hers.

"Tell me."Bird said to Emma.

"He was shot twice."

"Oh, my God," she had a catch in her voice thinking about Killian, "Two times. How is he?"

"The one in his leg went through the other side. They're doing surgery on the one in his side. That bullet didn't go through. It traveled. It's in a dangerous place, but the doctor is very confident that he can get the bullet out without harming anything close to it."

"What is close to the bullet?"

"Well, it traveled upwards, so it's close to his heart and major arteries. They worry he might bleed out before they can repair all the damage, but I talked to Killian. He said there was nothing to worry about. He isn't going to leave us. So let's not worry."

Bird shook her head and looked around. She spotted the

woman sitting there watching them. "Is that beautiful woman, the one Killian has guarded for the last month?" she asked. Kelly pulled on her hand, and she looked down. "What is it, sweetie?"

"I didn't feed my chickens."

Bird looked at Skye. "I forgot about my animals," she spoke, and a tear slipped out of her eye.

"I'll take care of the animals," Jonah said, putting his arm around Bird and hugging her.

"You will? Thank you."

He looked at Kelly. "Do you want to go help me? We'll take care of the animals until Bird can make it home."

"Bird, can I go with Uncle Jonah? I have to show him what to do."

"I guess. Jonah, make sure you remember to feed him."

"Who took care of you? Of course, I'll feed him. What about Gracie? I can take her."

"I'll keep Gracie with me, thank you. Kelly, I'll tell your daddy you are taking care of the animals for us. I'll call you tomorrow."

"Okay, come on, Uncle, my chickens, are hungry."

Bird gave him a big kiss. "I love you."

"I love you too, Bird. I love Gracie too."

"I know you do, sweetie."

Bird wiped at a tear as Kelly and Jonah walked away. Then she turned to Emma. "Who shot Killian?"

"It was the man who was after me. Emma killed him," Avery said, standing up. She walked over to the beautiful woman holding the baby.

Bird frowned. "I hope there aren't any more out there hunting for you. I can't believe your father-in-law hired a man to kill you."

"Well, he's my ex-father-in-law, and it didn't surprise me

at all. I'm happy to meet you, Bird. Killian told me about you and the kids."

"He did?" Bird said with a frown between her brows.

"Yes. Killian loves you very much."

"Did he tell you that?"

Emma and Skye both shook their head at Avery, but she wasn't looking at them. She was looking at Bird.

Bird looked at both of her friends. "Can you believe him? Why would he tell her he loved me? When he hasn't even called me in five weeks. Does he not know how he's supposed to treat the woman he loves?" she questioned. She was tapping her foot. "I'm pregnant. I swear to God, all he has to do is touch me, and I get pregnant."

"I'M sure he does more than touch you," Skye said with a grin on her face. "Congratulations."

Bird giggled like a schoolgirl. "I love that man. Sometimes I want to strangle him, but I love him."

Avery looked at Bird. "He called you. He thought you didn't want to talk to him. He left you messages every day. I heard him. I wasn't snooping, but sometimes he would leave three or four messages. If the shooter hadn't come close to getting me, he would have gone to Temecula and talked to you in person."

"I never got a call from Killian."

"Maybe he has the wrong number."

"So, the father of my children doesn't have my phone number."

"Bird," someone called out. She turned her head and saw Arrow, Lillian, and Brinley walking towards her. "How is he?" Lillian asked.

"He's going to be fine. I don't want you to worry. Killian

is too strong for a bullet to stop him. Let's sit over here, and you can play with your granddaughter."

Bird led Lillian to a chair and put Gracie on her lap. "Gracie, this is your grandma."

"Gracie, what a beautiful name. Hello, Gracie. Can Grandma give you a kiss?" Lillian asked. When Gracie heard the word kiss, she kissed her grandma.

"Oh, what a darling granddaughter I have," she looked at Bird. "Thank you, dear. I love her."

"Good because in eight months, there will be another one."

It got really quiet. Then they all busted out laughing.

"Good, the more babies, the better," Lillian said. I would like a house full.

KILLIAN FELT like he was flying to a beautiful place. There were colors everywhere, bright, beautiful colors. He saw his father and mother, then he saw Mary Jo. "Mary Jo, you're alive."

"No, Killian, I'm not."

"What are you saying?"

"You died, Killian. You are with us."

"No, I can't be dead. Bird needs me. I'm sorry, Mary Jo. I love her so much. She needs me. My kids need me."

"It's too late. You've died."

"No, I'm not dead. I refuse to die. Goodbye," he told Mary Jo. Killian looked around at his parents and Mary Jo. "I love you all."

THEY WERE in the waiting room when the doctor walked in. "We almost lost him, he died, but he fought like hell to live. He will be in intensive care for a few days, then he'll go to his own room. Two people can see him right now. They only allow two people at a time in there."

Bird looked at Lillian. "Would you like to see him with Arrow?"

"No, dear, I'm going to let you see him. I'm going to wait until he has a room of his own. I don't want to see him with tubes and wires all over him. I might have a heart attack if I see him looking like my mind is picturing him."

Bird looked like she might take off running any second. Arrow held his hand out to her. She stood there a few moments staring at his hand before she put her hand in his. Brinley took Gracie, and Arrow and Bird walked down the hall on their way to see Killian. Bird stopped walking a few times before they got to the door where Killian lay and almost died. They picked up the phone to the ICU, and a nurse buzzed them in. Bird felt like she was going to hyperventilate she was so nervous. She had to stop and make herself calm down. When she saw Killian lying on those white sheets with all of those wires and tubes, she grabbed Arrow's hand again. She cried out, and tears fell from her eyes. She was angry that Killian was here. How could this happen? He was in his backyard for crying out loud. She took the tissue Arrow handed her without saying a word. Then she looked at Arrow.

"I haven't talked to Killian in five weeks. But he has the time to tell the woman he was guarding that he loves me. Can you believe he hasn't called me, but he told her everything he should have told me?" she whispered in a grieving voice. Bird was getting angry because she knew she would break down and start crying. There wasn't a damn thing she could do about it. She spotted the only chair in the room and sat down.

"Are you going to be okay?" Arrow asked, handing her more tissues.

"Of course, I am," she answered. Bird kept crying. Arrow gave her the box of tissues. "Why would I not be okay? I have this handsome man who loves me. I mean, look at him. I could never find anyone who would run close to Killian. It's just," she sighed as she blew her nose, "why would he tell a stranger about me? My life is private, and for that woman to say to me, yes, he called you, he must have the wrong phone number. Bla Bla Bla. What do you have to say?"

"I'm just happy he's going to live."

"Of course, he's going to live. I never doubted that. He wouldn't dare die. I'm having another baby, for crying out loud. I've slept with Killian twice. Can you believe that? Twice, and I'm having another baby."

"Congratulations."

"Thank you," Bird calmed down a little. "I'm sorry, I don't do well with stress."

Killian could hear every word Bird was saying. She was always calm. Did she say she was pregnant? He remembered going to be with Mary Jo and telling her he loved Bird. Killian knew it scared Bird. She was afraid he would die. He had to do something so she would know he was here to stay. He tried to open his eyes, but he couldn't. He tried to say something to her, but he couldn't.

13

"When is he going to wake up?" Bird asked the doctor again. She'd asked him the same question every time she saw him. It'd been a week since Killian's gotten shot, and Bird couldn't figure out why he hadn't woken up. Besides, the woman who he was guarding wanted to go home. Ash told her she could return home when Killian said she could go home.

"He'll wake up when his body is ready to wake up. Don't forget we lost him a couple of times on the table. Why don't you get yourself and Gracie some lunch? I'll keep an eye on Killian." The doctor said.

"We brought lunch today. We'll eat our lunch in a little bit. I'm going to read Killian all the messages he got today."

"Okay, you do what you need to do. I'll see you tomorrow unless Killian wakes up, then I'll be back."

They had their lunch, and Gracie was tired. Bird picked her up and laid her beside her daddy, so she could take her nap. She had taken her noon nap with her daddy all week. She liked rubbing his back while she was going to sleep. Gracie would kiss her daddy on his back. Bird watched them.

She wished she could crawl up there beside them. Just to hear a voice, she talked to Killian as she had done all week. "Don't turn over Killian, Gracie is sleeping next to you."

"Okay," he mumbled.

Bird froze. "Killian, are you awake? Can you hear me?"

"What," his eyes opened once before shutting again.

Bird pushed the button for the nurse before picking up Gracie so the nurse could check on Killian. "Shhh, don't cry. Daddy's waking up. You can go back to sleep when the nurse leaves."

The nurse walked into the room. "Did you call?"

"Yes, Killian is waking up."

"Well, it's about time. Killian, can you hear me? Killian, can you open your eyes?"

Bird watched as Killian did nothing. The nurse looked at her with a pitiful look on her face. "Killian, answer the nurse this minute, or I'm going home," Bird said in a voice she would use on a stubborn animal.

"Okay, don't leave."

"Well, I see he is waking up. I'll call the doctor."

Gracie was determined to get back in bed with Killian, so Bird put her next to her daddy. She rubbed his back again to put herself to sleep. "Dada."

"Yes, it's Dada."

Killian chuckled. The doctor walked in at that moment. "Well, I see he decided to wake up. Killian, can you hear me?"

"Yes."

"How do you feel?"

"I feel good."

"Can you open your eyes?"

"Let me get the baby," Bird said.

"No, leave her where she is," Killian said.

Bird wiped her eyes because Killian wanted his daughter

to stay with him. Killian opened his eyes and looked at Bird. "Come over here, sweetheart."

Bird walked to him and cried.

"Why are you crying?"

"I'm happy. I didn't ever think you were going to wake up. I have so much to tell you."

"Can we hold off on that until I check Killian?" The doctor said as he checked Killian.

"I'm sorry, of course, you can check him first," she said. Then she looked at Killian without taking a second breath. "Killian, we're going to have a baby. Why did you tell a complete stranger you loved me when I didn't hear a word from you in five weeks?"

The doctor smiled. "We would all like to know the answer to that question."

Killian shut his eyes and went back to sleep. "I'm going to call his brother and tell him Killian is awake. There is so much to do now. I have to get back to my home and take care of my business. I can't have my friends running my business any longer. I need to have Jonah bring Kelly here to visit his dad."

Doctor Johnson smiled at Bird. The entire floor loved her; she even visited the other patients on this floor. One of the patients told him she went to his ranch and helped his mare have its colt. As he watched, she picked up Gracie and walked to the next room to let everyone know Killian was awake. She picked up her bag and walked out of the hospital.

Three days later, she still hadn't come back. Killian tried calling her a few times, but there was no answer.

"Killian, would you please tell Ash I can go home now. I don't need anyone to guard me; the guy is dead. Emma killed him," Avery Talbot said with her hands on her hip.

"Why is she still with you?" Killian asked Ash.

"I thought you would want to be the one to make the decision to end the contract."

Killian frowned. His mind was still on Bird, and her not answering her phone. "I now end the contract. Good luck, Avery. It was nice knowing you. Has either of you talked to Bird? I've been calling her, and it goes to voice mail."

"You have the wrong phone number. I told Bird you left messages those five weeks she didn't see you.

"What, do you mean you told her?"

"Bird was upset when you got shot. I heard her telling Skye and Emma that you hadn't called her in five weeks. So I told her I heard you leaving messages on her phone. I also told her you loved her very much. I don't think Bird liked me telling her, but I had already told her," Avery shrugged her shoulders.

"What the fuck is her phone number?"

Ash pulled his phone out of his pocket and looked up Bird's number. He told Killian, and Killian looked disgusted with himself. "I can't believe I've been leaving messages on the wrong phone all this time. God, that means she hasn't gotten one message from me in all the time I've known her. Fuck, I better call her and explain why she has never gotten a call from me. How did you get her number?"

"We all have it. Bird gave all of us her phone number. I'm guessing she did it in case you needed it."

Killian laughed. "Did she tell me she was going to have a baby?"

Avery grinned. "Yep, and you've only done it twice."

"That's not true. We may have only been together two nights, but we've done it dozens of times."

Ash and Avery both laughed out loud. "I'm going home today. I'll be back to work in a couple of weeks."

"Well, I guess this is goodbye, guys. If you ever need a private investigator, give me a call."

"Take care, Avery, and don't go making any more father-in-laws angry."

"I'll try not to. Good luck with Bird, Killian," Avery said, walking out the door.

Ash looked at Killian. "I thought they said you could go home next week."

"I'm leaving today. I'll ride back to the house with you and get my truck. I'm off to Temecula."

KILLIAN PULLED into the driveway of Bird's property and knew right away, something was wrong. The animals were louder than he'd ever heard them. Bird's vehicle was where she always parked it. He ran up the front steps and opened the door, calling her name as he went through the house. The baby's diaper bag was on the sofa. *Where the hell is she?*

He called Jonah on his phone as he walked through the house.

"Hello."

"Have you seen Bird?"

"Not since she got home the other day."

"Her truck is here, but there is no sign of her or the kids. Gracie's diaper bag is on the sofa. The animals are all going crazy."

"Have they been fed?"

"How the hell do I know? I know absolutely nothing about animals," he said. Killian leaned against the counter, and his eye caught a piece of paper, he picked it up. "Fuck, fuck, and fuck."

"What?" Jonah bellowed.

"There is a note. It says, *'When I get mine, you can have yours.'* Jonah, it's written in blood. How the hell did he get the blood? What does it mean? Shit. Hang on, someone's calling."

"Hello."

"Daddy," Kelly cried, "he keeps hurting Bird."

"Kelly, honey, who's hurting Bird?"

"A mean man," Kelly cried like someone did something to him.

"Kelly, honey, can you put Bird on the phone?"

"No, the man said you didn't know that there were two," Kelly replied, then the phone went dead.

Killian tried calling the number back. He couldn't get through, so he called Jonah back.

"Hello, what the hell is going on there?"

"That was Kelly. He said a mean man has them, and he's hurting Bird. Kelly said we didn't know there were two."

"What the fuck does that mean?"

"Son of a bitch. I think he has to be talking about Avery. Her father-in-law hired two men to kill her. Not one," he explained. Killian mentally made a list of what he needed to do. "Get the guys and Avery and come here as fast as you can." Killian felt like he was going to fall down; his side was throbbing.

Killian paced until the noise from the animals caught his attention. He went out and started feeding them. An hour later, a helicopter landed in the pasture where Bird was going to put more horses. He watched as the Seals and Avery jumped out.

"Have you heard anything else?"

"No. I think the guy is testing us. How did he know I was out of the hospital? I wasn't supposed to be out for a few more days. He must have called, and they told him I checked myself out. So if that's what happened, maybe he took them today."

Avery looked around. It felt like no one had been here for a few days. "As much as I hate saying this, I don't think Bird and the kids have been here in a few days. It's like he was waiting for her. Gracie's diaper bag is still on the sofa. I've only known Bird for a couple of weeks, but I don't think she would leave the bag on the sofa all this time."

"She's right. Bird wouldn't leave it out," Jonah said, picking up the bag. He looked inside and spotted her phone. "Why would she put her phone in here?" he wondered out loud. He walked into the kitchen and plugged it into the charger. When it came on, he checked it out for messages. Killian had left like ten of them. With the last few being from here, there was a sense of panic in his voice. When he looked at her photos, a man in the living room was the first one to pop up. He could tell she took it at a strange angle. So this was why she put her phone inside the bag. He handed the phone to Killian with the photo.

"Do you think he took them?" Jonah wondered out loud.

"Why else would she take a picture of him? Of course, this bastard took them," he growled. He passed the phone around so everyone could look at the photo.

Killian walked over and stared out the window. He saw something pink on the ground and walked outside. He bent down and picked up a pink napkin. On it, Bird wrote, *I love you*. Bird left him this message. He folded it and put it in his pocket. Killian decided right then he would frame that little piece of paper, and keep it on his nightstand. He walked back into the house. "I'm going to send this picture to Brinley. She will be able to bring everything about him up on the computer. I'm going to kill this bastard."

Bird was more frightened than she had ever been in her life. This man had no soul. She looked into his eyes, and they were empty. That was what scared her the most. Her grandmother could put a curse on him, but she was in Louisiana. Bird tried keeping the kids quiet so the man wouldn't get angry. Every time he became angry, he would punch her. Bird didn't cry out; she didn't want the kids to see how frightened she was. Kelly was so brave, trying to protect her and Gracie. He promised her he would always take care of his sister. Bird didn't worry about the baby in her tummy. She would keep it safe.

"It's time for you to call your dad, again, except this time he'll know for sure I mean business. Call him."

Kelly sniffed as he called his dad. He didn't want that man hitting Bird anymore. Kelly looked at Bird, and she smiled, even though her lip was bleeding, and her eye kept getting blacker and more swollen. He looked at Gracie, who was behind Bird. That's where he was until the man told him to call. Bird made them stay behind her. He dialed his daddy's number.

"Hello, Kelly, honey, is this you?"

"Yeah, Daddy, he told me to call you again," Kelly spoke. Kelly watched him go to Bird and punch her in the face. "Leave her alone!" Kelly screamed at the man. Killian could hear Gracie crying, "Daddy, please make him stop hitting Bird," Kelly begged. Kelly threw the phone down and bit the man on his leg. The man picked him up and threw him against the wall.

Bird attacked the man. "You get your filthy hands off my son, you disgusting bastard. I'm going to put a curse on you."

Killian was shouting into the phone. Everyone heard the entire conversation. The phone was on speaker. "I'm going to kill you. You son of a bitch. Do you hear me? You fucker, pick up the fucking phone."

The man knocked Bird back down and grabbed the phone. "Who's more important to you, that bitch or this little

Bird and her babies? I'll give you fifteen minutes to decide who will live."

"You listen to me, you son of a bitch, you lay one more finger on my family, and you will suffer before you die," he threatened.

"To late, I already did lay my fingers on them."

The phone went dead but not before he heard Bird scream.

"Fuck!" he roared at the top of his lungs. He hit the wall, and a giant hole was next to a picture of Louisiana that Bird had hung on the wall.

"Calm down. We have to have a plan," Ash said. Jonah stood at the window, saying nothing.

"I have a plan," Killian said. He looked at Avery. "I will not allow my family to ever get hurt again."

"I know. Tell him he can have me as soon as you get the kids back. That way, he will give you the kids. He will not let Bird go until he has me. Once you have the kids, I'll walk over and change places with Bird."

"No," Jonah said, "he'll kill Bird anyway. We have to figure out where he's hiding them. It has to be around here somewhere. Have you heard from Brinley?"

"No," Killian roared. "We can't stand around waiting. If there is a chance I can get my kids, I'm going to take it. It will be easier to rescue Bird if she's not so concerned with them. He'll continue to beat her because he knows how much it hurts the kids. I say we let him have Avery for the kids, and that's what we will do. It's my family. As long as he has Bird and the kids, he'll keep hurting her."

"Killian, you are no longer our lieutenant. We are equal now. You can't decide what we are going to do. We vote on what we do." Ash said, looking at Avery.

"I vote to save my kids right now."

"Damn it," Jonah nodded his head. "I hope he agrees to the switch. And doesn't kill any of them."

"We'll find out soon what he's going to do," he said. That's when the phone rang. Killian answered it. "I have a trade for you."

"I'm not interested in trading. If you want me to kill your family, don't do as I say. If you want them to live, then give me the woman."

"Give me my kids, and you can have her."

"Don't you fucking tell me what to do? I tell you what to do."

"Then fuck off," Killian said and hung up on the crazy bastard.

"Why did you hang up?" Jonah demanded.

Killian held his hand up. The phone rang. "Daddy, he said you better get us in twenty minutes, or he's going to kill Bird. The lady has to stay there. We'll be at McDonald's," he said. The phone went dead.

"Someone GPS McDonald's, let's go." He looked at Avery, "Good luck!"

She nodded, and they walked outside. Ash brought up McDonald's on GPS, and he stepped on the gas. Killian didn't take a chance on being late. When they pulled into McDonald's parking, his kids were sitting alone at an outside table. Kelly held his sister on his lap. His phone rang.

"My gun is pointed at the little Bird's head. When I see the woman, I'll let you get the kids."

Killian looked at Avery. She nodded once and stepped out of the truck, prepared to get shot right then. But no shot came. Instead, the kids walked to Killian, and she walked to where the kids were seated. Kelly looked at her when she walked by. Avery winked at him to let him know everything would be okay.

Killian picked them up and held them to his heart. Both

of them were filthy, but they were alive. That was all that mattered. Gracie's diaper was full. He took it off of her and wrapped his shirt around her. Jonah drove home while he held his kids. When they got home, Brinley, Arrow, and Emma were there. Killian squeezed the bridge of his nose to keep from crying out loud. He had to use his brain right now and plan. Brinley took Gracie from him, and Arrow picked up Kelly.

"KELLY, you are so brave. Do you know how proud we are of you? Wow, look at you. I bet you got these bruises from helping someone."

"Yeah, that mean man kept hitting Bird, and I bit him on the leg. Then he threw me into the wall," he sniffed and wiped his nose on his sleeve, "Bird jumped on his back and pulled his hair." Kelly looked at Arrow. "Bird said he doesn't have a soul. She said his eyes were empty. That's what Bird said," he sighed. He started crying. "I don't want him to hurt Bird anymore. I love her. She said I could call her Mommy. Is that okay, Daddy?"

"Yes, son. I would love for you to call her Mommy," he answered. Then he walked to the horse corral and cried.

"What's your plan?" Brinley asked, standing next to him.

"Avery is going to try talking him out of killing Bird. She's going to convince him that a professional killer doesn't kill people who don't need to be killed."

"She better convince him. Bird has gone through enough since I've known her. She survived a serial killer. I'm sure she will survive this fucker."

"I hope so; I can't lose her. I died while I was having surgery. I saw Mary Jo. I told her I couldn't go with her. I told her I loved Bird, and I was staying here on earth with her. I can't lose her."

"If Bird gets his gun, she's a crack shot. She told me her dad would take her and Jonah hunting. Bird said she killed nothing, but she could shoot anything her dad or Jonah pointed to."

"That's for sure. She could out-shoot anyone in our community," Jonah said, leaning against the fence. "Bird will do anything to save the baby."

The baby, Killian, forgot all about the baby. *What have I done to my family? I brought this monster to my family, and they are the ones paying*. He walked back into the house, where he picked up his daughter and called Kelly to come to him.

"I love you two more than anything in this world. Kelly, thank you for taking care of Gracie and for standing up for Bird. You are so brave. Do you know where he has Bird?"

"Yep."

"What! You know where they are?"

"Yep, they're in a house behind McDonald's."

Everyone stood up and looked at Kelly. "Someone has to stay with the kids," Killian said.

"I'll stay with the kids," Emma offered. "Go!"

BIRD WATCHED AS BUTCH, the hired killer, pushed Avery into the room. "Where are my babies?" Bird demanded to know.

"They're with their father. I don't kill kids."

"No, but you don't mind hitting them," she spat and looked at Avery, who had said nothing.

"You can let Bird go now. You have me; I'm who you want."

"This little Bird isn't going anywhere. Get your ass over there next to Bird. We're leaving this place. Both of you walk, and don't try anything stupid."

Bird wasn't about to try anything. She couldn't let

anything happen to her unborn baby. She gave thanks to God for keeping Gracie and Kelly safe.

"Why do you need Bird? You already got paid for my death. She has nothing to do with this."

He pointed the gun at Bird's head. "I'll kill her right now if you don't do what I say. Bird, you go first. Avery, you walk behind her but not too close. I need to have an excellent shot at her head."

He already had handcuffs on Bird when she got inside his car. He turned to Avery and hit her on the back of her head with the barrel of his gun. She fell. He caught her before she hit the ground. Butch pushed her in the car's backseat and put handcuffs on her.

"Why did you do that? She's bleeding. You hurt her."

"That's what they hired me to do. Did you forget I'm going to kill Avery?"

"No. I didn't forget. How could I forget you've told me a hundred times?"

"Aren't you going to thank me for releasing your kids? I was close to killing that brat. That's why I let them go."

Bird looked at the killer. He told her his name was Butch Lancaster, and he'd been in the business of killing since he was eighteen when his father kicked him out on the street. Butch hired a guy for fifty dollars to kill his parents. He was the ugliest person Bird had ever seen. Not because of his looks. It was because the devil was in his soul. His eyes looked black, like they went straight to hell.

"Do you really do curses? I have a couple of people I would like to put a curse on. My ex-wife is one of them. If I could find her, I would kill her and her new husband. I almost did once, but she lived. That was a disappointment, let me tell you."

They were driving down the freeway, and Bird felt tears wetting her face. The further they got down the highway, the further she got away from Killian, Gracie, and Kelly. *Will I ever see them again? Yes, I will. I'll make sure of it.*

"Why do you want to kill me?"

"I'm not going to kill you, Bird. I'm keeping you because you're my insurance, so your husband won't start shooting. He won't take a chance at killing you."

"Killian is not my husband."

"He's not. Why not? You're the mother of his children."

"I'm not Kelly's mom, only Grace's and the one I'm carrying."

"So you're pregnant, and he hasn't asked you to marry him. Sounds to me like he doesn't want to marry you."

"That's not true. Killian loves me. I'm not talking to you about Killian. You need to do something for Avery. Her head won't stop bleeding."

"Well, if she dies, then my job's over."

AVERY WAS AWAKE, but her head hurt like crap. She thought she might vomit any second. Avery listened to Bird talk. When she first got a look at Bird, it made her sick with all the bruises on her face. She had to get them away from him before he killed both of them. Avery knew he wouldn't let Bird go free.

KILLIAN KNEW before he kicked the door open, they were gone. They most likely left as soon as he got Avery. He looked around and saw Gracie's blanket. It had blood on it—*Probably Bird's blood.* "Bird," he whispered while holding the blanket to himself. Kelly said the man hurt her. He walked outside, and Brinley was on the phone. Killian walked to her.

"Ryker says his name is Butch Lancaster. He's wanted by every law enforcement agency in the United States. He hired a guy for fifty dollars to kill his parents when he was eighteen. Since then, he's killed so many people they lost count. His dad, who didn't die but is in hiding, said he doesn't have a heart or a conscience. He has hundreds of disguises."

"Do they have an address?"

"Nothing."

"Where could they be?" Killian asked anyone who could answer him. No one said a word.

"Do they have an address for the other guy?"

"Let me check."

She hit a button and started talking. "Ryker is going to call us as soon as he finds it."

"We might as well head back home. Or do we want to hit the road, hoping to see them driving? I'll bet he lives around Los Angeles, so we can go that way. Even when Ryker gets an address, we'll be closer to it. I can't wait around for something to happen to Bird. The blood on Gracie's baby blanket tells me he enjoys hurting her," he snapped. He looked around. "Let's hit the road."

They piled into the Suburban and took the freeway towards Los Angeles. Brinley called Emma and let her know what was going on.

An hour later, they stopped for gas. Killian was praying the cashier would know something when he asked him a question. "Have you seen an ugly guy with two women?"

The man nodded his head. "Yes, yes I did. I called the police, but they didn't come here. I wrote the license plate," he told Killian. He reached under the counter and handed Killian a piece of paper.

Killian was in shock. He couldn't believe the guy answered yes. "How long ago was this?"

"Maybe forty-five minutes."

"Did you see the women?"

"One woman. She has blonde hair and bruises. She went to the bathroom, and a lady came out and brought me this," he replied. He took a paper off of the shelf behind him.

Killian thanked him as he rushed outside. "Ash, you drive," Killian said, jumping in the passenger side. He explained what the guy told him, and then he read the piece of paper.

"Help us, tell them I love them."

"Bird wrote this. A woman brought it from the bathroom. The cashier called the cops, and they ignored what he told them. He said he told them the blonde girl had bruises on her face and arms."

"Did he say how long ago that was?" Arrow asked.

"Forty-five minutes. If he's driving the speed limit so he won't get pulled over, maybe we'll catch up. His car is black. Keep your eyes on all the black cars. He read off the license plate to them.

14

Bird felt a pain in her stomach. She rubbed it and spoke quietly to herself and her baby. She promised him a good meal when they were free of this man. *"Baby, if I can get that gun, I'll kill him. I won't let him hurt you.* "Avery, I won't let him kill you either," she whispered. Avery turned her head and smiled. Avery couldn't raise her head, or she would start vomiting all over. Bird smiled back.

JONAH COULDN'T BELIEVE they had to find one car on this damn freeway. "This is ridiculous. These freeways are packed with black cars. We'll never find them. How the hell are we supposed to find one car out of thousands?"

"Just keep driving, Ash. We'll look for the car. All you need to do is drive. We will find them. I'm sure Bird realizes we're following them. She'll do something for us to find them."

"I'M GETTING CAR SICK. Being pregnant makes me more nauseous than normal." Bird said, looking at the back of the man's head.

"Keep your hands in the car, and don't try to bring attention to yourself. I can see you in my rearview mirror. I'm sure you remember how much I enjoy hurting you."

"How could I forget when I can't talk without hurting?" she growled. Butch laughed so hard, he started coughing. Bird prayed he would choke to death. At least he rolled the window down. If, by some miracle, Killian was behind them somewhere, maybe he would see her. She looked over at Avery. She didn't look so good. "I think Avery needs some water on her head."

"Don't tell me what Avery needs. I told you, I don't care if she dies. I'm going to kill her anyway."

"You've already been paid. Why can't you just let Avery go?"

"Because I'm a professional hitman. I make sure my job is done. I haven't touched that money. When Avery is dead, I will spend the money. Until then, it stays in my account. I'm taking a trip to Italy next week. I have to kill a family there, so I thought I would vacation while I'm there."

"You're killing an entire family? That's horrible. Those poor people. Why would someone want them dead? Are there children as well?"

"Yes, there are five children."

"But you said you don't kill kids."

"I don't. The woman who hired me will be the one who strikes the match. I'm going to set up their home, so when they are asleep, they will all burn to death."

"Why does she want them all dead?"

"Because she married into this family to become rich. She told me she didn't realize that the older brother had control of the funds. Stella said she couldn't get him to raise their allowance. I guess she tried begging him for more money. He told her she married his brother for the family money, and she was lucky he gave her anything."

"Why would she tell you all this?"

"You would be surprised by what people tell you. Most of them tell me about their life stories. It takes the guilt off, if they have any, to begin with."

"Why are you telling me?"

"I guess you figured out I'm going to have to kill you too. So what does it hurt to tell you about Stella Rossa? I'm booked up for two years. I have this one guy who has been dating a woman for six months. He's going to pop the question and ask her to marry him. Frank says all the sick stuff he does to her, she will never turn him down. Then all he has to do is get an insurance policy on her, and he's a rich man."

"I hope they catch you and fry your ass for what you've done. Do you really think I would let you kill me? I have my child to guard. You'll die before I allow you to hurt my baby."

Avery reached over and touched Bird's leg, trying to get her to shut up. She wished she didn't feel like she would die. Her head felt like it was split in half. She was no help to Bird. Avery couldn't even open her eyes. Her head was spinning so fast.

"DAMN IT, Bird, you're making me angry again. You've pissed me off for the last time," he reached around and slugged her in the face.

Bird had had enough of this fucker. She threw her arms around his head and pulled with all her might; she was going to choke this bastard. He was fighting to breathe, and she was all the way on the floor of the car. She noticed Avery reach her arms over his head also. She was trying to help Bird, but that made it worse. Avery's handcuffs cut into Bird's hands, and she screamed out in pain. Avery removed her cuffs, but it was too late. Bird could no longer pull hard on her cuffs. Her wrist hurt too much.

Butch pulled her hands away from his head and pulled the car over. "You're going to die now, bitch!" he shouted.

He drove down a dirt road into a field off the freeway. Bird didn't know it, but they were being followed. When he pulled over, he pulled Bird out of the backseat and knocked her to the ground as the other vehicle pulled up with the tires squealing.

Killian jumped from the vehicle and threw himself on Butch. He hammered his face with his fist. When Killian was finished, he pulled Butch up off of the ground.

"Arrest this man before I kill him!" he shouted.

Bird watched as Killian held his side. There was blood on his shirt. Bird knew this man had to die. If he didn't, then he would keep on killing families. Brinley stood next to her with her arm around Bird.

Bird took Brinley's gun from its holster and shot him between the eyes. Arrow cussed, seeing everything, and Brinley took her weapon from Bird, putting it back where it belonged; she strapped it in a holster. "I had to kill him. He was too evil."

Brinley put her arm back around her friend. "Don't worry about killing him. He deserves everything he got."

Killian walked over and pulled her into his arms. "Thank God you're alive," he said with relief. He kissed her lips. "How about we head home?"

"Yes, let's go home. Avery's in the backseat; she needs to go to the hospital."

"Thank you guys for showing up when you did; he was

going to kill me and then Avery. I pissed him off one too many times."

"I love you," Killian said as he kissed her.

"I love you too," she replied. Bird then got right down to business. "We need to find his book, the one he keeps all of his appointments in. He has a list of people who he's been hired to kill. One of them is an entire family in Italy. I think he has someone helping him. The lady who hired him wants the family she married into murdered, all of them. Her name is Stella Rossa. I think you should call and have her arrested right now," she said, looking at Brinley.

Brinley nodded and took out her phone to alert the officials in Italy.

Killian couldn't take his eyes off of her face, neck, and arms. "If he wasn't dead, I would kill him with my bare hands for doing this to you."

"Killian, it's alright, it'll go away. All of my babies are safe now; that's all that matters. I'm starving. Do you all have anything to eat?"

Ash handed her a bag of chips and a Pepsi. Bird was in seventh heaven even if it burned her lips. She licked them when salt got on the cuts. She started to shake as she thought about killing that man. *He had to die.*

"Damn, it Bird. You will be the death of me if you keep getting into these spots of trouble. You get out of one and into another. What am I going to do with you?" Jonah asked, looking at her poor face.

"Can you open this Pepsi for me? My hands are so sore?"

That's when they noticed the handcuffs on Bird's wrist.

"Fuck, let me see your wrist?" Killian demanded. "What the hell did he do? Did he twist the cuffs while they were on you?"

"No, that's why he pulled over here to kill me. I tried choking him while he was driving."

Ash had taken the keys out of the dead man's pocket. He walked over and took the cuffs off of Bird, and he touched the cuts and kissed her wrist. Before backing away at a look from Killian.

"Thank you, Ash," Bird said, blushing. "Avery has them on her as well."

Brinley helped Avery stand; she was so dizzy, she couldn't stand on her own. As Bird watched, Avery started vomiting. Bird took her the rest of the Pepsi.

"Drink this, Avery; it'll help."

Avery nodded and drank it slowly.

"Does that feel better?"

"Yes, thank you, Bird," she smiled. "I have never known anyone like you. You are so brave. I'm sorry, I couldn't help you."

"We're safe, that's all that matters, and you traded places with my babies; I will owe you forever," she thanked her again. She looked around. "I don't know about you guys, but I would love a shower right now. Here Avery, eat the rest of these chips. The salt will help your stomach."

Brinley smiled the entire time Bird talked.

Bird looked at her. "Did you get his address? We have to make sure the family is safe."

Brinley nodded her head. "Do you ever stop?"

"Yes, when everyone is safe. I don't know how you all can be agents and protect the world. It would drive me frigging crazy thinking about all the ones out there I don't know about."

All of them except Avery busted out laughing. When the police pulled onto the road, dust flew everywhere. They still laughed. Killian and Jonah went to talk to them. Brinley and Ash were still grinning.

"What's so funny?" Avery asked.

"When I first met Bird, she used herself as bait to catch a

serial killer who was killing girls for some ritual. Then there was Katy. Bird picked her up, hitchhiking. Bird hid her from her step-dad, who had killed her mom because he wanted to marry fifteen-year-old Katy. I have to admit, he was a sick son of a bitch. Bird got shot at that time and almost died."

Bird frowned at Ash. "They were friends of mine. Some of them died. I had to stop that bastard. And Katy's step-dad wanted her for sex," she looked at Avery, "he poisoned her mother. I'm sure you would have done the same thing."

"I don't think I would ever pick up a hitchhiker, but I'm glad you did."

"But it's all the time, Bird. You are always rescuing people and fixing animals. You have to take time and have this baby before Killian turns gray-headed."

"I promise, I'm not going to get into any more trouble," she assured her friend. Bird turned her head and looked at her best friend, waiting for her to come to her rescue. "Brinley, please say something."

"The hell with Killian turning gray-headed. My hair is turning gray."

"You two are impossible," she groaned. Bird walked to where Killian was speaking to the police.

"Can we take some photos of your injuries?" they asked Bird.

"No, Killian will take them and send them to you," she looked at Killian, "can we go home now?"

"Yes."

They climbed into the SUV and headed back to Bird's house. Brinley looked at her friend and smiled. "Arrow and I are going to look for a place close to you. Can you believe we're moving here?"

"What, that's wonderful. I'm so happy. When are you going to look?"

"Tomorrow."

"Really. Dang, I wish my face wasn't so messed up, or I would go with you."

"I'll send you photos of the houses we look at. It needs to be big and grand-looking. I wish I could find one that looks just like my home in DC. Did I tell you Ryker is buying my house? So at least I don't have to get a realtor there."

Bird sighed. "I know the perfect house for you?"

"You do?"

"Yep. Let's drive by it on our way home?" she asked. Bird heard Ash chuckle but ignored him. Then the others chuckled, even Avery. She ignored all of them. "Ash, when we get close to the house, I'll tell you where to turn."

"Okay, sweetheart, but don't you think you should see a doctor?"

"No, I don't think I need a doctor," she replied. Bird looked at Avery. "I'm sorry, Avery. Do you want to stop at the hospital first?"

"No, I feel better now. I'm anxious to see this house you're talking about. Then I'll see a doctor."

"Good. 'Brinley, I think you'll love it. When Katy, Gracie, and I saw this house, I thought of you. I would never have dreamed you would move here."

"I'm excited to see it. Arrow wants to live near his brother, plus my mom lives in California now, so this is the place for us."

They were close to Bird's house. "Turn left up here, Ash. When you get to the next street, make a right. Brinley, close your eyes. You guys don't say anything. Here it is. Arrow help Brinley out," she instructed. Brinley was a little clumsy, getting out with her eyes closed.

"Okay, open your eyes," she said. Bird watched as Brinley opened her eyes. A massive grin came on her face.

"It's beautiful," Brinley said as she ran up the front steps to look in the windows of the old Victorian home.

"I know where the key is."

"Where is it?"

Bird grinned. "Under a flower pot in the back," she answered. They all walked to the back of the house. "I found it when Katy and I were looking at it."

"It's fabulous. Arrow, look at this place."

Arrow smiled, then he put his arm around Bird and kissed the top of her head.

Brinley flew from room to room. She was now in the master bedroom upstairs with Arrow, with an enormous smile still on her face. "Look Arrow, it has a little bedroom connected to our room. We can put our baby in there."

"What, baby?"

"Our baby."

"Are you saying you want to have a baby?"

"No, I'm saying we're having a baby."

"What, are you pregnant? We're having a baby!" he shouted to everyone in the house. He picked her up and twirled her around.

"Hey, congratulations, you two. I'm so happy for you," Killian said.

Brinley beamed. Bird grabbed her side as a sharp, stabbing pain shot through her.

Brinley rushed to her. "What's the matter? Is it the baby?"

"No, it's nothing. Please don't tell Killian. He'll only worry. If I keep having things happen to me, he'll never ask me to marry him."

"Are you telling me he hasn't asked you to marry him yet? Damn, he's slow."

"I am not slow. I was going to ask Bird to marry me when we are with the kids," he defended. Bird screamed and held her side.

"What's wrong, sweetheart?" Killian picked her up and looked into her face.

"Nothing is wrong. I only had a little pain," she said before she fainted.

"Oh my God, what is happening? Bird darling, please wake up. She's burning up," he groaned. Killian didn't know what to do. "Please don't die. Bird, wake up, honey," Killian pleaded. He gently shook her, then he walked her downstairs. "Ash, start the car. We have to take Bird to the hospital."

"What the fuck happened to her?"

"Just drive," he hissed. They were all quiet, driving to the hospital.

"What the fuck happened to her? Is it the baby?" Ash demanded to know. "She needs someone to take care of her. She's accident-prone, and things happen to her."

Killian sighed. "Ash, you've asked me the same question five times!"

"Killian, please don't shout. I'm fine. It's just a little after-effect from being with Butch. Please don't worry. Ash, I am not accident-prone."

Killian held her close. He couldn't breathe. His whole body shook, thinking something terrible was going to happen to her. "I don't want you to die. Bird, I love you more than I've ever loved anyone. You're my whole life. Please don't leave me," he pleaded. Killian didn't care who heard him.

"I love you too. Will you marry me?"

Killian chuckled, as Bird knew he would. "Yes, I will marry you."

"Ouch," Bird screamed as Ash pulled into the emergency entrance.

Ash jumped out of the vehicle and shouted for help. "We need some help here! Something is wrong with Bird!"

Killian ran past him carrying Bird, calling for a doctor as

he went through the door. "Bring her over here," a familiar voice said, throwing a sheet over the bed. "Bird, what brings you back in here?"

Bird opened her eyes and smiled. "Hello, Doctor Benjamin, how are you?"

"I'm waiting for you to tell me what the hell happened to you? It looks like someone beat the hell out of you."

"A fucking mad-man kidnapped her and our kids. Bird is pregnant and in a lot of pain. Can we tell you the story later?"

"Where is the pain?"

When he asked, pain shot through Bird. She screamed and squeezed Killian's hand.

"Don't let her die."

"I'm going to do an ultrasound on you. Killian, you may as well go to the waiting room. This could take a while."

"Doc, can you have someone check on Avery? The killer hit her in the head with a gun. She was knocked out for a long time and was pretty sick when she came to."

He called a nurse over. "Can you go to the waiting room and check on a woman there? Her name is Avery."

"Yes, I'll go right now, doctor."

"Isn't that nurse your sister?"

"Yes."

"Why does she call you doctor and not Benjamin?"

"Because I call her nurse," he smiled, thinking about his sister.

When the test was over, it was what doctor Benjamin thought it was. "You've got a high fever, Bird. Your appendix is inflamed and could rupture at any minute. I'm going to take you into surgery and remove your appendix."

"Okay, will you have someone tell Killian? Tell him I'm going to be fine. Well my baby be okay?"

"Your baby will be just fine. I've already sent word to Killiant; the nurse is going to prep you for surgery. You'll have to have anesthesia now, the baby will be fine, so don't worry about anything. We need to get you in a gown. The nurse is on her way. I'll see you when you wake up."

"Hurry, it's really hurting."

15

"What's taking so long? They've been in there for hours."

Brinley turned and looked at Killian. "She's been in there for forty-six minutes."

"It feels like hours."

"Why don't you call Austin and see what's going on with your business?"

Killian walked outside and did what she said. "Hey, Austin, how's it going there?"

"How's Bird?"

"She's in surgery still."

"That family Brinley talked to, the Rossa family? The head of the family wants to talk to Bird. I told them she was in surgery."

"Why does he want to speak to Bird?"

"He wants to thank her. Storm and I found Butch's book with the names of his victims. This guy has killed hundreds of people. We have their names and the names of who hired him to kill them."

"Wow, I wonder why he kept something like that? He

must have wanted everyone talking about him. He probably thought he would be in the history books of bad guys. He loved himself, is what Bird said."

"This guy lived in luxury. Zane Taylor got in touch with his father and told him his son was dead. The guy cried. He said this was the first time in twenty years that he's felt safe enough to go out and buy groceries."

"What have we got coming up?"

"Do you remember the country singer? Shay Tanner. The guy we caught has been set free. So she called us. She wants you to call her."

"Did you tell her I'm busy? I'm not leaving Bird. I don't care what she says. Someone else will have to stay with her. Why the fuck did they release him? The fucker pulled a gun on her? He threatened to kill her."

"Shay said the police didn't read him his rights or something stupid like that. She's terrified. She's at her brother's in Louisiana, but she's afraid he will hurt her nephews."

"Should I bring her here?"

"Yes, can you stay there with her?"

"Only for a week. I have to be in France next week. Guarding that visiting politician."

"Maybe Ash can stay with her. I'll talk to him, he's in the waiting room. What else is going on?"

"I would have called you today, but I didn't want to disturb you while everything else was happening. Two kids have been kidnapped. Their parents believe it's the husband's mistress. It took a lot of questioning before he broke down and mentioned the mistress. His wife completely freaked out. She told me she thought they were happy together. She said they weren't having any problems. The husband was scared to death. He said Martha, who is the mistress, can be strange. He told me she liked anything he did to her and would do whatever he wanted her to. He broke it off with her because she started doing even weirder sex stuff. She has been doing crazy stuff since he broke it off with her. She threatened to kill his wife and kids. She sneaks inside their home when they are gone. Instead of calling the cops, he decided to handle it himself. So this is what happened with him handling it himself."

"How old are the kids?"

"The girl is ten, and the boy is thirteen. He said he's scared she'll rape them because she has a sick sex drive."

"How long have they been missing?"

"Since yesterday morning. Storm is already on it. And I had a call from Rhys Cohen."

"What's Rhys doing these days?"

"He quit the Seals. I told him to come here when he's job hunting."

"Did he say why he quit the Seals?"

"I felt like it was something he didn't want to talk about."

"Can you keep me informed on the kids? I'll tell Ash about Shay; maybe he won't mind keeping her safe. I'll call you after I talk to him."

"Okay, I hope Bird can stay out of trouble for a while."

"You and me both. I'll let you know when the wedding is."

"It's about damn time."

Killian walked back into the hospital, looking for Ash and Jonah. It was time to get back to work. "Ash, do you remember Shay Darwin?"

"Sure, I do. You kept Shay safe until we caught the guy who threatened her life."

"Well, she needs our help again. Because of some mess up, the guy was set free."

"What the fuck is wrong with people. Where is she?"

"She'll be in Los Angeles soon. Austin is going to watch over her for a week, then he has to be in France," he said. He went on to tell them about the kidnapped children, and that

Storm was following some leads, but he needed help. "The woman who most likely took them is crazy, so we need to find them fast. Jonah, when can you go?"

"As soon as I know about Bird. Where do they live?"

"They live in Portland, Oregon," he replied. He told Jonah about the husband and his mistress.

Jonah shook his head, muttering something about crazy dangerous idiots. "The quicker we find them, the better. I'll give Storm a call."

The doctor walked into the waiting room, and everyone stood up. "Bird is doing great. She's sleeping and will probably sleep for the rest of the night. So all of you should go home and get some rest. I'm sure the kids will be happy to see you, Killian. You can come back in the morning."

"I want to see Bird, then I'll go home and shower. But I'm coming back and staying the night right here with Bird."

"Follow me, and I'll take you to her."

Killian walked down the hall beside Doctor Benjamin, knowing the doctor wanted to let him have it. He waited, and sure enough, he was right.

"I don't want to see Bird here one more time looking like this. Her entire body is covered in bruises and cuts. If you can't keep her safe, then get the hell away from her, and I'll keep her safe myself."

Killian stopped walking and looked at the doctor. He took a step closer and growled deep in his throat. "I will keep Bird safe. You stay the hell away from what's mine," he turned and walked down the hall, then stopped. " We're getting married, you know. Are you coming to our wedding?"

The doctor chuckled, "I wouldn't miss it. Don't stay long. Bird really does need her sleep."

"I only want to check on her."

When Killian was inside the room, he looked at Bird, and

his heart jumped in his throat. "Hey baby, I love you. I'll be back after I shower," he kissed her cut lips, then her forehead, her fingers. He kissed every bruise he could see. Killian promised her he would keep her safe always. Then he walked out. Doctor Benjamin was there to make sure he left.

16

Killian pulled his kids on his lap. "I want you to know Mommy is going to be fine. She'll be coming home tomorrow. Bird can't wait to see both of you. She wanted to come home today, but her doctor wouldn't let her. When she comes home, we have to take care of her," he was telling them, but Gracie wasn't listening to him. She was climbing all over him. She started kissing his face.

"Dada."

"Yes, darling, I'm your Dada. Thank you for the kisses."

Gracie climbed on her brother, and kissed him, then she sat on his lap. "Bubu."

"Yes, Kelly is your brother," he looked at Kelly. "I see your sister loves her brother. Do you enjoy living here with Bird and Gracie?"

"Daddy, this is our home. My mom and my sister live here. I love living here. Please let's never leave."

"We will never leave, this is our home, and Uncle Arrow and Aunt Brinley are moving close by us."

"I know, Uncle Arrow told me already."

"Does he tell you everything?"

"Yes, he does, especially if it's something that important. Are you going back to the hospital?" Arrow said. Walking into the room.

"Yes, Bird wants me to wash her hair. Do I look like a beautician?" he asked sarcastically. He looked at his son, who giggled, and his daughter farted and laughed. "I hope you outgrow this farting behavior, young lady," Killian said, throwing Gracie in the air.

Arrow laughed. The more Killian made Gracie laugh, the more she farted. "Damn, what did she eat?"

"She ate beans and cheese," Kelly said, waving his hand in front of his face.

"You two behave for Uncle Arrow. I'm off to wash Mommy's hair."

"Tell my mom I love her."

Killian handed Gracie to Arrow and picked his son up. "You are so brave, and you are the best son anyone could ever have. I love you so much."

"I love you too, Daddy."

"KILLIAN, please help me shower. I haven't had a good shower since I left my house. No one will ever know we are in the shower. We'll be so quiet."

"What if I get soaked? They will all know it because I have no dry clothes to put on."

"You can take your clothes off. No one will know."

"Are you crazy? What if Doctor Benjamin walks in? He's already said he will kick me out of here if I don't behave. I swear the guy wants you. He told me if I couldn't keep you safe, then he would."

"That's so sweet," Bird said, getting out of bed.

"Where are you going?"

"I'm taking a shower. Come on, you can wash my hair. You might want to take your clothes off."

"No, Bird, please don't make me do this. You know we'll get caught."

"They've already checked me for the night. We'll leave the light over the bed off, and they'll think I'm sleeping. Wash my hair and back. I feel dirty. My hair hasn't been washed in over a week. I can't do it myself because my body hurts too much. Come on live dangerously. Doctor Benjamin has gone home for the day."

"Okay, but if the nurse walks in, I'm blaming you." he gave in. He helped her into the bathroom and turned the shower on. After fixing the temperature, he undressed. "I'm leaving my boxers on."

"Damn, you're a sight for sore eyes. I love how sexy you look. There are so many things I love about you. I bet you thought it was the sex I loved about you. That's a huge part, but there is a lot more to you than sex."

"Bird, don't start that. I'm washing your hair and your body for you, and then we are getting out of the shower."

"If you say so. You know how much I love you touching me?"

"Bird, stop it. You have so many bruises I'm afraid I'll hurt you."

Bird giggled. "You won't hurt me."

They walked into the shower and stood under the spray of water. "Killian, do you remember the last time we took a shower together," her voice was husky.

"I will never forget that. It was four in the morning. I fell in love with you that night," he confessed. Killian put shampoo in his hand and lathered her hair. It was so long, he needed more shampoo. He stroked her back with the shampoo.

There were so many bruises; he saw red. Bird leaned

against him with her eyes shut. He looked at her and smiled. Bird was sleeping standing up. He rinsed her off, then he wrapped the towel around her. The other towel, he used for her hair. Killian picked her up and carried her to the bed. He stopped when he heard a noise out in the hall. He was dripping water, and his boxers clung to his body. *Damn, I hope to hell no one comes in here.*

Killian put Bird in the bed and then wrapped the towel around himself. He put her hospital gown back on and wrapped her hair with a dry towel where she wouldn't get wet. Then he went back to the bathroom and dressed. He threw the boxers in the garbage. He bent his head and kissed Bird goodnight, then he yawned and crawled in beside her.

"Shhh," Bird whispered as a nurse walked into the room the next morning. "He has had no sleep in over a week."

The nurse nodded and whispered back, "The doctor said you can go home. Should we wake Killian and let him know?"

"Oh, he's so comfortable."

"I'm awake, sweetheart, and I'm ready to go home," Killian spoke then. He looked at the nurse. "Thank you for taking care of Bird. We are getting married in four weeks, we would love for you to be there. I'll drop your invitation off as soon as we get some made up."

"I would love to go to your wedding. Thank you for asking me. I'll get the papers for you to sign, and you can go home."

As soon as she left, Bird turned and cuddled closer to Killian. He put his arms around her and pulled her closer. "Birdine Brewer, will you marry me? I love you so much, I never want to be away from you again."

"Yes, I will marry you. I love you. I want to spend the rest of my life with you."

"Okay, get up. We are going home. My mom is coming to

visit us. Arrow is picking her up at the airport. Do you mind if she stays a while?"

"No, I love your mom. The kids will enjoy her visit. You should ask her if she wants to move here. I mean, she's all alone, I'm sure she has friends, but you're her only child."

"I'll talk to her about it while she's here."

The nurse came back into the room then. "Here you go. If you sign these papers, you can go home."

"Thank you."

"MAMA, I'm so glad you could visit. I've missed you, and so has Kelly. And look at your granddaughter. She loves you. Gracie, don't climb on your grandma's head."

"Well, I was going to talk to you about that. I've already been looking for a place to live. I've found a condo in town, I haven't seen it in person yet, but I have seen many pictures. I love it. It is two bedrooms which are perfect for Hazel and me. She has no one in Washington DC anymore, so she's moving here with me. And when I'm gone, she can spend the rest of her life there. She's packing the personal things I'd like to bring with me, she'll be here tomorrow. Which is something else I wanted to talk to you about? If you and Bird have any time, I would like for you to go through our home and take what you want."

"Have you already taken what you want?"

"Yes, everything I want will be here tomorrow. And the movers will unload my furniture and arrange it for me."

"You've been busy. I'm so happy you're moving here. When do you want to go to see your house?"

"How about tomorrow morning? I heard Arrow and Brinley are also moving here. We'll all live near each other. Now, how is Bird doing? Kelly told me that the horrible man beat her. I'll cook dinner tonight. In fact, I'll order our pizza now."

Killian laughed and kissed his mom's cheek. When it was her turn to cook dinner, he remembered that she always ordered pizza or Chinese food. "Bird's sleeping, she wanted me to wake her, but she needs her rest."

"I've had plenty of rest. Hello Mama, you look beautiful."

Lillian stared at Bird. "You poor dear," Lillian jumped up and hugged Bird. "If that man weren't already dead, I would kill the bastard myself. Come sit down, darling. I told Killian I bought a condo in town, and Hazel and I will be living there. When the two of you have time, you can go back to my home and take whatever you want. I've taken all I need."

"I'm so excited you'll be living here. We'll have so much fun. I know you're tired, but do you think you can help me plan my wedding if you have a chance? Did Killian tell you we're having another baby? So I would like to get married before I start gaining weight."

"I would love to help you, dear. Why we should have Hazel make you a dress. She made Mary Jo's wedding dress, and it was beautiful, wasn't it, Killian?"

"Yes, it was, but that was another life. Bird is going to have Brinley go with her to Santa Barbara. They have beautiful wedding gowns at a boutique there."

"Of course, I'm sorry. I don't know what I was thinking."

"It's okay. You can mention Mary Jo. I'm not going to break down and cry every time I see that guilty look on Killian's face. I know she was Killian's wife and Kelly's mother. I know she was graceful and beautiful, and I know I'm neither. I'm always getting into trouble. My problem is I think I can save everyone. I feel sad that Mary Jo died at such a young age. But I'm going to be Kelly's mommy now. I love him as if he was my own. I want him to think of me as his mommy."

Killian couldn't believe Bird thought he felt guilty. "Bird, I don't feel guilty for being with you. I love you more than I have ever loved anyone. You're both beautiful and graceful. I'm proud to have you as my wife. I have never wanted anyone as I want you."

"Killian," she whimpered. Bird knew she was going to cry, but she couldn't help it.

He stood up and brought her to her feet. "You are the only woman I ever want," he softly kissed her lips.

"Your mom's going to think I'm a crazy idiot. I'm sorry, maybe I am tired. I need to call a friend of mine from Louisiana and invite her to our wedding. I'll see you at dinner. Arrow is cooking for us tonight. He's a superb cook," she complimented. Bird turned and walked out of the room.

"Me and my big mouth. I'm sorry, Killian. Should I go speak with her?"

"No, don't worry about it, Mom. Bird is tired. Look, Mom, Mary Jo was before, and Bird is now and forever. I don't want Mary Jo's name brought up anymore. I don't know if it hurts Bird. She would never tell you if it did because she is an angel who would never tell you if she was hurting. The love I have for Bird is stronger than any love could be."

"Hey, Shay, it's me, Bird. Call me. I'm getting married. You said if I was ever lucky enough to marry anyone, I better invite you. It's in four weeks, so keep that week free. I also have some terrific and sexy songs for you," she told her. Someone knocked on her door. "Come in," Bird called. She smiled as Kelly came into her room. "Hey, sweetheart, what have you been doing?"

"Playing with Gracie, she's sleeping now. Can I lay down with you?"

"I would love that. Come over here. I remember how you saved me. Thank you, Kelly. I want you to know I'm so lucky to have you for my son. I love you. We're going to have so much fun as a family."

"Yeah. Aunt Skye was going to teach me how to ride a horse. Can you teach me instead?"

"Yes, as soon as I'm able to ride a horse, I'll teach you," she answered. Bird smiled as Kelly crawled next to her and cuddled close. His eyes were already closing, and so was hers.

Killian was looking for Kelly everywhere when he decided to check Bird's room. When he opened the door, he smiled. Both of them were curled up next to each other, sleeping. He quietly shut the door.

17

Bird's phone wouldn't stop ringing. She got out of the shower to answer it. "This better be good. I was in the shower," she spoke. Bird heard giggling. "Hey, where are you? I'm getting married in one week."

"I miss you too, Bird. I'm in hiding. A crazy man with a gun is trying to kill me."

"I'm sorry, I do miss you. Do you still carry your gun?"

"No, my agent didn't think it was a good look for me to have a gun in my purse."

"That's crazy. Go buy yourself a new one right now. If that creep gets close, you can shoot him. I have some songs for you."

"Can you please sing one of them for me? I've been so depressed lately."

"Are you coming to my wedding?"

"Yes, are you getting married in Louisiana?"

"No, I live in Temecula, California, now."

"What, I can't believe you left Louisiana. Why would you move to California?"

"Some things happened back home. I wanted to get away from all of it."

"I'm sorry, Bird. I heard about what happened to you. I will be there tomorrow. Now can you sing me one of the songs?"

"Let me get my guitar," Bird got up and dug around in her closet until she pulled out an old guitar. She brushed it off with her hands. It had an inscription on it that read, *To my little Bird who sings like an angel. Love you, sweetheart. Daddy.*

Bird ran her hand over that word *Daddy.* She wished he was here to walk with her on her wedding day. "Are you still there, Shay?"

"Yes. Do you still have the same guitar?"

"Yes. This song is about a love so strong when he died, he refused to go to heaven. Until his love could go with him. She didn't know that he was still with her until he saw her going to end her life, then he showed himself," she responded. She began to sing the song that could be heard outside because the slider door was opened.

Killian and Brinley walked toward the voice. "Who is that? I love that song. It's so beautiful," Brinley said, walking toward the house.

"That's Bird. She always sings to Gracie and me," Kelly said, standing by the slider.

"Bird sings?" Killian asked.

"Yeah, she likes to sing. But not too big, people. Only Gracie and me."

Killian watched her through the screen. Her voice was so powerful, and the song was beautiful and sad. He saw her wipe a tear off her cheek.

"Are you crying? Because I am. Bird, you have to sing this one. It's made for you. Oh my God, Bird, you have to sing this one. Please at least think about it. It's a number one hit."

"You know I don't have time to be a singer, that's why I write them for you. Not only do I have an animal hospital, I have two babies and one on the way."

"Damn, Bird, no wonder you're getting married. Don't you remember when your dad gave you that guitar? He said, Bird, you go out there and show the world how good you are. Why can't you just sing one of your songs for your dad? You write so many."

"Because I don't sing in front of people. Please quit asking me. Call me and let me know what time your plane arrives. I'll pick you up. And get yourself a damn gun."

"Okay, I'll get one today. Love you."

"Love you too."

"Bird Brewer, how come I didn't know you could sing?" Killian asked through the screen of the sliding door.

"Because I don't like singing in front of people."

"I told you, Dad. Mom is shy."

"You should have let me know you were listening."

"I was listening to you sing. Your voice is amazing. I don't understand why you would hide that voice. It was so beautiful. So you write songs?"

"Yeah, I only used to write them for my friend, and then I started writing for more artists. It surprised me that they even wanted my music. This doesn't mean I'm going to start singing for you all. I'm still shy."

Killian had a look on his face she didn't understand. "What? I know you have something going on in that head of yours."

"It's nothing. I'm surprised that you never mentioned that you are a famous songwriter?"

"I wouldn't call myself a famous songwriter. I never thought about the money. I write for relaxation. I don't write for the money. We haven't had a lot of time alone to even talk much. There are things you don't know about me, and there are things I don't know about you. But we are getting to know each other."

"Do you make a lot of money?"

"Yes, I guess I do."

"Don't you know what you make?"

Brinley butted in on the conversation. "I loved it, Bird. It was beautiful. You should share that beautiful voice with others. But only if you want to. So an old friend is coming to your wedding?"

"Yes, she'll be here tomorrow. I haven't seen her in years. But we promised each other that we would come to each other's wedding. No matter how long it's been since we saw each other."

"But you write songs for her."

"Yeah, I've been writing songs for her since we were in high school."

"IT'S the song that makes a singer famous, so if you write all of her music, then you made her famous."

Bird giggled. "She writes most of her music," she informed them and changed the subject. "I'm going to teach Kelly to ride a horse today. Are you ready, Kelly?"

"Yes!" he started jumping up and down. Acting like he was riding a horse.

"Let me see if Gracie is awake."

Brinley stepped inside. "I'll watch Gracie. You teach Kelly how to ride a horse."

Killian hadn't had so much fun ever that he could remember. Bird had Kelly on the horse in front of her, teaching him how to ride. He was so excited his face turned beet red in the sun. He wanted to cry from happiness. He loved Bird so much. He refused to feel guilty because he was so happy with Bird, and so was his son. He hoped Mary Jo would understand he loved her. Now he loved Bird.

Bird looked at Kelly, grinning. "Are you ready to try on your own?"

"I don't know?"

"I'll be right here beside you the entire time. I won't let go of the horse. I promise."

"Okay."

Bird walked Sally around the corral a few times. Kelly's grin never left his face. Killian was taking pictures. She would make faces, and he would laugh. She hadn't felt this happy in a long time. Bird made one more round and stopped. Killian took Kelly off the horse.

"Was that fun?"

"That was super fun! Can I do it again?"

"Yes, if we have time tomorrow. Don't go around the animals unless your dad or I am with you. Okay?"

"Okay, I won't."

Bird kissed him on his cheek. "I love you, and I want you to be safe."

"I love you too."

Killian threw his arm around Bird. With his other arm, he carried Kelly. His life was perfect. He had his children and the woman he loved right where he wanted them. Gracie was talking up a storm to Brinley. You still couldn't understand her, but she was like her mommy. She loved to talk.

"Well, I'm afraid I've got to run. Arrow is busy remodeling the kitchen. I told him I would bring him a cheeseburger and fries. And you know how Arrow is with his food."

Bird shook her head and laughed. "Thank you for everything. I can't wait until it's finished. I'm sure it will be beautiful."

"Tell him I'll be over there tomorrow morning to help," Killian promised.

"I'll tell him."

18

"I'll take Kelly with me," Killian said. "He wants to help the men do construction today. I'll see you this afternoon. The family will arrive today. Can you let me know when they show up?"

"Sure, I might have to leave to pick up my friend. She said she would call me when her plane landed. Skye, Lucas, and Dakota are going to be here later. Two more days, are you getting cold feet?"

"No, I will never get cold feet, I love you, and I can't wait for you to be my wife. Let's go back to bed."

"We can't. We have a little boy standing over there waiting for you to take him to Uncle Arrow's."

"Come on, Dad."

"Here, I come," he said. Killian kissed Bird goodbye and turned and picked his son up. "I'll see you later, sweetheart."

As he got in his car, Bird's phone rang. "Hello,"

"My plane will land in forty-five minutes. Are you going to meet me at the airport?"

"Shay, I'll leave right now," she replied. Bird went into Gracie's room, "Come on, sweetheart, we are going to pick up my old friend. Shay Darwin is going to love you," she told her. As Brinley was backing out of the drive, Skye and her family pulled up. "Hey. I have to go pick my friend up. I'll be back in a couple of hours. Killian and Kelly are at Arrows. They are helping him with some remodeling."

"We'll go check their place out and catch up to you later."

"Okay, see you then."

KILLIAN ANSWERED his phone when he saw Ash's number pop up. "Hey, Ash, what's happening?"

"I've lost her."

"What do you mean?"

"She tricked me. Shay used her pillows in her bed so I would think she was sleeping."

"Why would she do that?"

"We don't exactly get along. Shay tried demanding that you guard her. I sort of told her you were getting married, so she couldn't have you. She got mad because she said I thought she wanted you for herself."

"Damn, Ash. I don't know how you could argue with Shay. She never argued once with me."

"That's because she likes you. She doesn't like me."

"Why doesn't she like you?"

"I told her she was a spoiled rich kid. She said I know nothing about her life, so I had no right to make assumptions."

"Well, you need to find her before the crazy fan finds her."

"She bought a gun."

"What do you mean she bought a gun? Why the hell did she do that?"

"So she could shoot the guy if he came after her."

"Damn, does she even know how to use a gun?"

"She told me she did."

"I don't have time to hunt for her."

"I'm following all the leads I can follow. I'll call you if I hear anything."

BIRD SPOTTED her as soon as she saw the woman with a walker. Shay was famous for disguises. Bird laughed when she pushed her way in front of a couple of men, then she acted like she needed help. One of them helped her by taking her arm.

"There's my granddaughter. Thank you for helping an old lady when she needed you."

"Anytime," the man said, looking at Bird. "Hey, Bird. I didn't know your grandma was coming to your wedding."

"Ryker, Ethan, it's good to see you two. Are you staying at our place?"

"No, we will be at Arrow and Brinley's. We're going to be putting up security as she had in D.C. Plus, he wants us to help do some construction in their new home."

Bird laughed. "He's taking advantage of everyone who's coming to the wedding. Do you want a ride?"

"No, we rented a vehicle."

"I'll see you two later," Bird turned and hugged Shay. "You are so convincing. You should have been an actor."

"Are you kidding me? It's bad enough being a singer. You can't go anywhere with everyone taking your photo. I have to make sure I have make-up on all the time if I go out as myself."

"You've never needed to wear make-up. You have long black lashes, and you've always been beautiful."

"I love being around you. You have always been the beauty in our high school group. Look at you. You're shining with happiness. Let me see this baby girl. Oh, Bird, she's magnificent. I love her—Gracie Mae, what a beautiful name."

"Thank you, let's get your suitcase?"

"I only brought this carry-on bag. It has all I will need in it. Besides, it's easier for me to grab if my bodyguard shows up."

"Why don't you want your bodyguard to show up? He's there to guard you. Did he know you were coming to my wedding?"

"I sort of snuck off."

"Then why did you hire him?"

"I wanted the other one."

"Why, was he better looking?"

"No, this one is just as cute, but this one makes me nervous, for some reason. I've missed you Bird, what the hell has been going on with you. My aunt said your granny told her you almost died a few times."

"YEAH, I've got myself in trouble a few times."

"You always thought you could save the world."

"I know, I've learned my lesson. No, more getting in the middle of trouble for me."

"Now, tell me who those men were."

"Ryker Reynolds and his brother Ethan, they own a high-security business. What happened with the guy who is after you?"

"I guess he's still after me. I haven't seen him anywhere. But at least if he shows himself, I'll be ready."

"You got yourself a gun?"

"Yep. And that was another thing that made Ash angry..."

"Wait, is he Ash Beckham?"

"Yes, do you know him?"

"Yes, he's an ex-Navy Seal he and some other ex-Seals

have a bodyguard business. Killian is one of them."

"Killian was my last bodyguard. You know him?"

"Yes, we are getting married in a couple of days."

"You're marrying Killian Cooper."

"Yes."

"Lucky you. Ash told me he was getting married. I'm glad he's marrying you. Do you think I should keep my disguise on?"

"No. I'm going to call Ash and let him know where you are. He'll worry himself sick trying to find you."

"Go ahead, but he better not be mean to me, or I'll run away again."

"I'll be sure and tell him what you said."

"It's beautiful here. It reminds me of Napa with all these grape fields. How long have you lived here?"

"Not very long, about four months. I love it here. I miss my granny, and she's so stubborn she won't fly on an airplane to visit me. I'll visit her after the baby is here. Jonah lives here too."

"That's good. Does Jonah work with them since he was a Seal?"

"Yeah, they all work together."

They pulled up to the house, and Shay was in awe. "Well, here we are."

"Bird, I love it. Do you have horses we can ride?"

"Yes, I had all of my animals brought here. Plus, I board horses for other people. Follow me, and I'll show you to your room. Then I'm going to call Ash."

Ash answered on the first ring. "Who is this?"

"Ash, it's me, Bird. I wanted to tell you Shay is at my house. I'm sorry she snuck away from you."

"How do you know Shay?"

"I went to school with her."

"Are you the one who advised her to buy a gun?"

"Yes, she knows everything there is to know about guns. Why shouldn't she have a gun if that guy comes after her again?"

"Because she's an idiot. That's why."

"Ash, she is not an idiot. Shay is brilliant."

"I've never seen that side of her. I'll be there in a few hours," he said, then hung up the phone, cussing up a storm.

"Is he angry?"

"Yep, he's angry. Hey, Shay, while you're here, let's not mention me singing, okay."

"Sure, why not?"

"Because I don't want to sing around other people. Killian and Brinley overheard me singing, and Killian wanted to know why I never mentioned it to him."

"Why didn't you?"

"It just never came up. So many things have happened since I met Killian. I guess I didn't want him to see how many things I always have going in my life."

Shay bent her head and looked at Bird. "Bird, you are one of the best singers I know. It's not just something you have going on in your life. You should be proud of how great a singer you are. Your dad was very proud of you. They walked into the main area of the home, and Shay stopped in her tracks. Who do those two belong to?"

"This is Lucy and Ethel. They belong to Brinley."

"I met her. She came over to the Seal house in Los Angeles the last time I was there."

"Is that what they call it, the Seal house?"

"Yeah. Didn't you know that?"

"No, Killian and I haven't had a lot of time to talk about much. We are both so busy. After we get married and get some things cleared up, we'll have more time together."

"Bird, make the time. That's what happened with James and me, he was so busy going all over the world, and I always had concerts all over the States. I loved him so much, but not enough to follow him in his career, and he didn't love me enough to stop going all over the world."

"I'm sorry. I remember when you came back home with a broken heart. I thought you two got back together."

"We did for about a month. Then his agent contacted him about going overseas at Christmas. We had already planned to go to Lake Tahoe to get married. All I can say is thank goodness I didn't marry him. He's already had three wives."

Bird laughed. She stood up when a house full of people walked in. Brinley, Arrow, Skye, Lucas, and Killian were laughing over something Skye said. When he saw Shay, he stopped and shook his head. "So this is your school friend?"

"Yes, everyone, this is Shay Darwin," she turned to Shay and introduced everyone. She looked at Killian. "I already called Ash; he's on his way here."

Killian pulled her into his arms and kissed her. "Shay, Ash said you carry a gun. You're going to have to give it to me."

"Why, is she going to have to give it to you?" Bird asked.

"Yes, why?" Shay asked.

"Because guns are dangerous," he replied. All four women looked at him like he was crazy. "What I mean is Shay is a singer. She hasn't been around guns. She'll end up shooting herself."

"That's crazy, Killian. Shay grew up shooting guns just like I did. We both hunted alligators and pheasants."

"Okay, so you know how to shoot a gun. Don't shoot anyone."

"The only person I'll shoot is the man who wants me dead. And Ash, if he keeps making me angry."

"You just be careful."

"Are we all ready to eat? I have the steaks ready. Did Kelly eat lunch?"

"Yes, darling Kelly had lunch," he answered. He looked

around for his son, but he couldn't see him. "Where is Kelly?"

Bird felt panic. "I didn't see him come in with you, and Gracie is sleeping."

They all walked outside to see where Kelly had taken himself off to. Bird knew right away where he was. The gate to the bulls was open. She ran to the gate and didn't think about throwing herself in front of Kelly if she saw a bull charge him. Killian shouted so loud the bull and Bird both stopped. "Bird, get the hell out of there!" he yelled. That's when Kelly came running from the barn. He had his red tee-shirt on, and the bull snorted, and his hoof pawed the ground. Killian ran towards Kelly, but he wasn't close enough. Bird knew she was. She shouted at the bull and ran as fast as she could. She grabbed Kelly up and threw him right into Killian's arms. The bull caught her on the side, then Killian was there. He kicked the bull full in the face and picked her up. Arrow and Lucas made the bull go back into its corral. "Sweetheart, are you okay?"

"Yes, thank you for saving me."

"I would die if anything happened to you. You are my life. You know that, don't you?"

Bird took his face in her hands. "Yes, I know that. Now let's feed our company."

"Bird, I'm going to look at your side while Killian gets the steaks out. Killian, bring her to your room." Brinley said, looking at her friend.

"Killian, you can put me down. I can walk."

"No, I enjoy carrying you," he countered. Killian saw the anguish come over her face. She cried out.

"No, my baby."

"Bird sweetheart, what's wrong? Talk to me," It tore his heart out when she screamed in agony.

"My baby," she cried.

Killian ran to the truck. "Arrow, you drive," Killian

shouted. "Brinley."

"I'm behind you."

Bird was screaming in pain. Thank God, it didn't take long for them to reach the hospital. Doctor Benjamin met them as they ran into the emergency room. "Over here. What happened?"

"It's the baby!" Killian shouted.

"My baby. Please, Doctor Benjamin, save my baby."

"Bird, what are you feeling?"

"I'm having lots of pain where my baby is."

He looked at Killian and Brinley. "You two need to go to the waiting room."

"No," both of them said at the same time. Killian bent and kissed Bird. "I love you, sweetheart. Everything is going to be okay. I promise."

Bird nodded before a sharp pain made her curl herself into a fetal position. She knew nothing was going to be the same; her baby was injured, and she did it. If she lost this baby, it would be her fault. She did it.

The doctor gave her something to put her to sleep, Killian wouldn't leave. Brinley sat on the other side of the bed. She wouldn't leave either. Her best friend was going to need her when she woke up.

"I should have made sure Kelly followed me inside the house. Why didn't I make sure he followed me? My child is dead because I wasn't paying attention."

"Listen, Killian, I know this must hurt you so much. Bird is going to need all of us. I called Skye, and she is taking care of everything at home. We both know Bird. She's going to do something. I don't know what, but something. I'm going to go home, tell her yourself. I'll be back tomorrow morning."

Killian nodded his head. He had been thinking the same thing. It was their wedding day in two days. He would talk to Liam, Emma's husband who was a pastor. Killian thought he would tell him they might have to put it off for a few days. But that was all. He wouldn't let her put it off any longer than that. He went to sleep sitting in the chair.

Bird didn't want to wake up. She knew when she woke up, her baby wouldn't be there. It was all her fault. She always tried to save everyone, and now her baby was gone. She touched her tummy, tears fell from her eyes, then she opened her eyes. Killian slept in the chair. This had to be hard for him. The baby was his too. She tried not to cry, but the flood gates opened, and there was nothing she could do to stop them.

Killian got up and crawled into bed with her. He pulled her into his arms and let her cry. Tears rolled from his eyes. He stayed there in bed with her until she cried herself to sleep. When he turned his head, his mom was there, sitting in the chair he vacated.

"How is she, dear?"

Killian shook his head. He couldn't speak, or he would cry.

"I'll just sit here for a while. Stay right where you are."

When Bird opened her eyes again, she was alone. Then Killian walked out of the bathroom. "Killian, I'm so sorry, I killed our baby."

"Stop it. You did not. This is not your fault. I should have made sure Kelly followed me into the house. I was so eager to see you. I forgot to see where he was. It's my fault. It's not yours."

"Stop, we can't blame anyone. Have you seen Kelly?"

"No, I haven't been home."

"Go, now he'll blame himself. We can't let him do that."

"I'll go soon. I'm waiting for your doctor. Kelly is with Arrow."

"Is it my baby doctor?"

"Yes. She'll be here in a while."

19

It's been almost a week since the accident with the bull. Bird cried all the time; she was sick at heart. Her poor little baby had to be strong, and she had to get past this pain in her heart. She had a family to take care of and a wedding. She walked through the house, hunting for Killian. She could hear him singing and smiled.

Bird walked into Gracie's room. Killian was singing to her while she laughed at her daddy. Bird smiled and started singing to baby Gracie with him.

"Mommy, sing."

Bird sat on Killian's lap. "I want Kelly home. The guy who owns the bulls is coming for them. So he won't be scared anymore. Let's go get him. Come on, Gracie, we're going to get baba."

Killian watched Bird. She was trying to get back to her usual self. "Are you okay?"

"Yes," she answered. She turned her head and kissed him. "I love you."

"I love you too, sweetheart."

"Tomorrow is the big day," he beamed. Killian hugged her as he carried Gracie, who had her head on his shoulder.

"Yep, I hope it goes smoothly."

Killian laughed out loud. "I can't imagine anything going smoothly with all the people we have for family."

"That's true. We have some pretty strange characters in our families."

"And our friends."

"Yes, we can't forget our friends," she said. Bird busted out laughing. "Are we mean?"

"Yes. And it feels good. Let's go."

"ARE you sure you don't want something blue on?" Brinley asked.

"Did you wear something blue?"

"No, but I think you need it more than most people," Brinley chuckled. "Sorry. Okay, then everything is set for the wedding. Are you ready? You look beautiful. I love the way Arrow braided your hair."

"I know, he's good. I love my hair. Well, I'm ready. You can go first. I'll leave after a few minutes to make sure you are up there where Liam is."

Bird heard Shay singing and knew it was time for her to walk out there where her friends and family waited. She took a deep breath and started her walk, praying she wouldn't trip.

Killian watched her, she was beautiful, he saw a strange look come over her face, he turned his head, and the man who was after Shay stood at the corner of the house. Bird stopped walking. "Hell no, he's not messing my wedding up," he growled. Killian stalked to where the man stood, took the gun out of his hand, and punched him in the face. He knocked him out cold. Then he walked back to where Liam, Arrow, and Kelly waited. Shay started back singing, and Bird began walking with a massive grin on her face. He knew she was ready to burst into laughter. When she reached him, he pulled her into his arms and kissed her until Liam cleared his throat.

The wedding only had that one interruption. The police came and took the man away. They made sure his rights were read, so it wouldn't get thrown out of court. The reception afterward was a blast. Shay talked Bird into singing her new song.

Bird was putting Gracie to bed when Killian came up behind her. He pulled her into his arms and kissed her. "I love you."

"I love you."

20

"Killian, we've only been married a week. Do you have to go?"

"Yes, there is a missing woman, and her brothers say she would never just go away without saying something to her family. Her car was found on the outskirts of town."

"Be careful. I hope you find her."

"You be careful too. I'm glad Arrow lives close by. Call him if you need anything."

"I will. I have a mare ready to give birth. Her owners want me to be there for the delivery. The kids are going to stay with Arrow when I'm needed."

"Give me another goodbye kiss," Killian pulled her to him. He loved the feel of her in his arms. He could hold her like this forever and never let go. She fit his body perfectly.

"HAVE THEY WALKED THESE ENTIRE MOUNTAINS?" Storm asked. Storm looked around at the ground to see if maybe the detectives missed something. He couldn't see anything except a lot of footprints.

"They say they did. But I don't think they looked everywhere. Her car was found at the lookout point. Her purse and phone were inside of the car, and it wasn't locked. I think she stopped to look at the view, and someone else also stopped. They must have taken her," Killian replied. Killian looked over at Storm. "It's been a while since I scaled a cliff, but I think that's what we're going to have to do."

"Yeah, it's been at least five years for me. The last time was when Ash and I went to Vietnam."

Killian walked to the back of the truck and took out the rope, two flashlights, and a backpack full of protein bars and water. He made sure the emergency medical kit was inside. He threw the pack over his shoulder and threw the rope to Storm. Who wrapped it over his shoulder.

"We'll go down as far as we can to see if there is any sign someone went this way."

"Lead the way. I'll follow you."

Killian looked down as he walked. It wasn't as steep as it looked. "It won't be as bad as it seems," he tried to be hopeful. An hour later, he changed his mind. "There is no one down here. Unless they brought a rope to help propel them down this damn mountain. I know her brothers think she would have jumped to her death rather than let someone push her into a vehicle."

"We might as well keep on going. We've come this far," Storm said. Storm looked around. "Why don't we make our way to that ledge over there. If it was me and I wanted to get away from someone. I would take my chances with this fucking cliff. I would climb down and hide. So yeah, let's look at all the ledges around here. We can find the overhangs to see if she's hiding under one. We'll check around here, then head on down the cliff. We'll go all the way down. That way we won't miss anything."

"Okay, but how would anyone be able to get to that ledge without some climbing equipment?"

"Hell, I don't know. Maybe she can fly," he joked. Storm reached up and took hold of a rock. First, he made sure it would hold him. He swung his body over until his foot found a protruding rock. He reached for another rock with his other hand until he could swing himself to the ledge. When he turned to see how big it was, he saw a woman's jacket. Killian landed next to him.

"What's that?"

"It looks like a woman's jacket, and I don't think it's been here for long."

"Maybe Ella Strong did come this way. Let's see if we can pick up our pace. Now that we can assume she went this way, she could be injured. She must have some rock climbing experience to make it this far," he stated. As they descended the cliff, they used their rope to propel themselves down. Killian spotted a woman's shoe and had a bad feeling in his gut.

Storm picked up the shoe and put it in the backpack with the jacket. "I don't think we're going to like what we find. If she just lost her shoe, then she would have put it back on. That would be the smart thing to do. She must have fallen, and her shoe came off. I think she's down at the bottom of this cliff. Why don't we call and have Ash bring the helicopter? He can see more with it than we can see from here. We'll keep going down, but he can be here in an hour. If we get lucky, he'll spot her and let us know where she is."

"That's a good idea," Killian agreed. Killian pulled out his phone and dialed Ash's number. "Ash, can you bring the helicopter?"

"Yeah, tell me where you are? I'll bring Rhys with me. He

signed on to work with us early this morning. I may as well start him out early. What are we looking for?"

"Storm and I are on the side of the cliff. We found a woman's jacket and a woman's shoe. We have a feeling we will find Ella Strong somewhere at the bottom of this cliff, hopefully alive."

"We'll be there as soon as we can. Be careful on that cliff. It's not a place you want to be scaling down."

"Well, fuck Ash, we figured that out after an hour. I wish I had known how bad this cliff was before I got here. That's why I'm afraid we'll find Mrs. Strong lodged between some rocks."

"Why don't you go back up until I get there?"

"I don't know where she is. We might find her before you get here. If she is alive, we can help her."

"Okay, I'll see you later."

He looked at Storm. "Rhys signed on. Is he still married?"

"No, he divorced his wife when he came back from overseas. Did you ever find out why he's not still a Seal?"

"No, I don't think he wants to talk about his reason for leaving. When he's ready, he'll tell us."

"Let's get going," Killian stated. Killian took a step down and almost tripped on a pair of women's sunglasses. He put them in the pack and kept walking. At one point, he had to grab hold of a rock and swing down to the next foothold. "Watch out; these rocks here are crumbling away. Don't step on any of them, or you'll slip and fall."

"Thanks for the heads up."

Frankie couldn't believe she fell. She had climbed cliffs all over the world. Why would she fall now when it was so important that she not fall? Her mom had to be here somewhere. Since she was a little girl, Frankie's mom, Ella Strong, had always told her, "If a stranger tries to grab you, you run. Even if he has a gun or a knife, you run. Because once he gets you in that vehicle, you're dead. So take your chance of surviving by running."

Frankie knew that's what her mom did. She ran. Her uncles hired a bunch of ex-Navy Seals to find her. If they were any good, they would climb all over the side of this mountain, hunting for her mother. They get paid an astronomical amount of money, and for what? To look at a damn computer. This was where her mother disappeared. This is where they would find what they needed to know. Frankie tried standing, but her leg was broken. She would have to tie it with a couple of pieces of wood. Thank God she didn't lose her backpack with her medical supplies in it.

Frankie Strong was a surgeon. She went anywhere she was needed to help children who needed heart surgery. She was a pediatric cardiologist. Sometimes she couldn't help a child. They didn't receive a heart in time. It was those times she would scale dangerous cliffs. She needed to be out there all alone doing something difficult. Sometimes she didn't know what to do, and that scared her. So she would take herself off where no one could find her. When her mom disappeared, she was gone on one of her journeys. Except for this time, she told her Uncle Thomas where she would be.

Some rocks rolled down the cliff right next to where Frankie sat. "Hello, is someone up there?"

"Did you hear that?" Storm asked Killian.

"Yes. Hello, keep calling out until we reach you."

"Just keep coming down, and you'll see me."

Storm followed behind Killian. Both of them stopped when they reached Frankie.

"Well, you're not Ella Strong," Storm said, looking at the beauty on the ground. Her short red hair curled around her face. Her eyes were the greenest green he had ever seen with long black lashes. Her lips were full and pink.

"If you are through gawking at me, can you find me a couple of pieces of wood so I can tie my leg up?"

"Who are you?" Storm asked as he checked out her leg.

"Who are you two?"

"I'm Storm, and this is Killian. Why are you out here by yourself?"

"I'm looking for my mother. My name is Frankie Strong. I'm assuming you are the ones my uncles hired to find her?"

Killian handed Storm two pieces of wood, and he opened up the backpack and took out some bandage and cloth. He wrapped it around the two pieces of wood and Frankie's leg.

"How does that feel?"

"It hurts like hell. But I'm thankful you did it, and I didn't have to. Thank you. Are you a doctor?"

"No, but I was a medic in the service. I know what I'm doing."

Frankie looked at the incredibly hot-looking guy, who was bent over, wrapping her leg, and for the first time in thirty-one years, her heartbeat accelerated to high speed. He was at least a foot taller than her. His shoulders were broad, and his light blue eyes looked at her like he wanted to devour her on the spot. The other guy coughed, and Mr. Blue eyes turned his head. *What the hell is the matter with me, thinking about this guy?*

"Why are you here by yourself?"

"Because I believe my mother is here somewhere on the side of this mountain. I don't know where she is, but I know she's here."

They heard the helicopter, and she looked around. "Is that your company helicopter?"

"Yes. Ash can see what's on the side of the mountain better than we can. But he'll be taking you to the hospital."

"No, let him look everywhere while the sun is up."

"Put your jacket on. Why the hell did you leave it behind? Put these on," Storm said, handing her sunglasses to her.

"There they are. I don't usually lose my belongings. I'm upset over my mom. She is an outdoor kind of person. But I don't know if she knows anything about climbing down the side of a mountain."

"If you had been smart, you would let us do our job, and you wouldn't have a broken leg."

"You listen to me, Storm, or whatever the fuck your name is. I've climbed plenty of mountains all over the world. I made a mistake, and I will take the credit for that. My mom is fucking missing, so don't tell me what the fuck to do. I'm not leaving this mountain until we've checked every nook and cranny on this damn giant ass rock!" she yelled. Frankie was shouting, and she didn't give a damn. It felt good screaming at someone.

Killian stepped in front of Storm before he could say anything else. "You can ride in the helicopter. Another pair of eyes will help us before nightfall."

Storm walked away to call Ash. "Hey, we have someone for you to pick up."

"Is it Ella Strong?"

"No, it's not Ella Strong. It's her daughter. She has a broken leg."

"I'll lower the basket when I see you, and you can strap her in."

"Okay, sounds good," Storm agreed. Storm looked over in the direction of Killian and Frankie. "Ash is going to lower the basket when he sees us…there he is," he said. Storm looked over at Frankie. "Why the hell did your parents name you, Frank?"

Frankie raised her chin a notch. "If you must know, my name is Francis, but my uncles called me Frankie from the time I was born. They liked making my dad angry. He passed away a few years ago."

Is that a tear? Storm couldn't believe she was going to cry. "Look, I'm sorry, I like the name Frankie. Please don't cry."

"I'm not crying over my name. I'm crying because I want my mom."

"Come here," Storm picked her up and held her close, and let her cry. "Are you ready to go in the basket now?"

Frankie wiped her eyes while this big, beautiful brute of a man cuddled her. She wanted to stay here with him. She looked at him. "Can you go with me?" she asked. She didn't know why she asked that question. She only knew she wanted him to stay with her.

"I can't. I have to stay here with Killian, Ash, and Rhys will be with you. I promise they'll keep you safe," he responded. Storm held her while Killian pulled the basket over to her.

"I'm sorry, I don't know what the hell is the matter with me?" Frankie said as she started to hiccup.

"You're worried about your mom. There is nothing the matter with you."

"Thank you. Please find her."

"If she's here, we'll find her."

Frankie nodded once. She knew if she said anything, she would beg to stay with them. She didn't want to leave here. Frankie knew in her heart her mom was on this mountain somewhere. She prayed they would find her, but why didn't she hear the helicopter.

Storm pulled her coat close around her. This woman made his heart hammer in his chest. The best thing he could do was to stay away from her. Before, he did something stupid like kiss her.

. . .

Killian and Storm moved further down the mountainside. It was slow going. They looked around every tree. They didn't want to miss seeing Ella Strong if she was here. Ash, Rhys, and Frankie flew all around the area hunting. Killian's phone went off. "Do you see anything?"

"No, but this damn woman needs a pain shot or something. She's in a lot of pain. I think she should go to the hospital. She's bossier than hell."

"No, I'm not leaving here until I find my mom. I'm alright. I won't say another word."

"Check in the medicine bag. There's some whiskey in there. Give her a shot of whiskey."

"Maybe that'll take away some pain," Ash said.

"Yeah, give me the bottle, and I'll pour my own drink," she said. Frankie took the bottle and took a drink from it before choking. When he tried taking the bottle back, she slapped his hand away.

When the sun started to go down, Killian told Ash to take Frankie to the hospital and head home and return early in the morning to resume hunting for Ella Strong. He and Storm would camp out for the night. "Storm, do you want a couple of these protein bars?"

"Yeah, I'll take a couple and some water. Thanks. What do you think about still hunting for our lady?"

"I think the family knows her better than we do. Who knows, we may find her. Whether she's alive or dead, I can't say. But it will give them peace of mind. I mean, look at Bird. She has been through some crappy situations this year, and she's lived through all of them. She's fantastic. God, I love that woman."

"Yeah, she really is something. Who would have thought you would marry Jonah's little sister? It sure is a small world we live in."

"It sure is. Hand me one of those blankets. The quicker we

get to sleep, the faster we get to wake up. I hope we find this woman. Her daughter would never forgive herself for breaking her leg. Women think they have to be the one who does everything. Frankie would think she would have found her mother if she hadn't broken her leg. That's the way their mind works."

"So because you're married, you know the way they think?"

"It's not because I'm married. It's because I know how the female mind works."

Storm laughed and turned over in his blanket. "Good night, mind reader."

"You can laugh, but I'm serious."

Storm chuckled before closing his eyes. It was just turning into daylight when he woke up. He sat up straight and looked over to where Killian slept. *Damn, he still gets up before daybreak.* He reached for his bottle of water, and took a long drink, and ate a protein bar before he heard Killian walking back to where he was. "Did you see anything?"

"No, so since we know she isn't to the left of us, we'll go to the right and pray we find her."

"Here, eat one of these."

"You know, Storm, it's times like these that I wish I would have gotten that second plate of food."

Storm chuckled. "I know what you mean. I never did like protein bars."

They cleaned everything up and started down the mountain. "Let's spread out more. If Ella Strong is here and can't call out to us, we'll have a better chance of seeing her."

"Good idea," he stated. Storm stopped and cocked his head. "I hear Ash. He's right on time," he said. When the helicopter got close enough to see who was with Ash, Storm growled. "Damn her. Why is she here? She has a broken leg."

"I told you women think nothing ever gets done if they aren't there to make sure it happens."

Storm ignored him. He kept walking, looking around the area, anywhere Ella could be. He stopped and looked at Killian. "How the hell could she have gotten around to this side of the mountain?"

Killian walked over and looked down the side of the mountain. "If you are a woman who is frightened for her life, you don't watch which way you run. You just run."

"Did you call Bird this morning?"

"Yes."

Storm chuckled, shaking his head. "You sounded just like her. Is she the one who told you women have to make sure it gets done?"

Killian laughed. "Yeah, she told me to go behind every tree. Because she would want to get behind a tree somewhere and cry. To me, it made sense. That's why we will turn over every rock."

"There are a lot of trees out here. We better get busy."

"We'll have some help. Ella's brothers and some others are starting at the bottom down there, working their way up."

They walked for hours. Both Killian and Storm's voices were hoarse from calling Ella's name. Killian's phone rang. "Hello."

"Hey, Killian, I need to refuel."

"Ash, how much longer do you think you can go without a fill-up?"

"Damn, Killian, I have a woman here with us. If I go down, I don't want her injured."

"How much longer?"

"Thirty minutes."

"Okay, you can fill…wait, I hear something," he informed Ash. Killian climbed back up from where he was. Storm ran over to him, and they both looked everywhere. "Ash, take the helicopter away. I can't fucking hear anything now," he snarled. Killian looked over at Storm. "There, did you hear that? Over there," they ran behind the tree, nothing. "I heard something. I know I did."

"Here," Storm said, looking into some brush. They pulled back the brush, and there was Ella Strong. Killian picked her up.

"Ella, can you hear me?"

"Yes. Be careful; I might have broken something. Who are you?"

"Your brothers hired our company to find you."

Storm was on the phone with Ash. "We found her," Storm notified him. He heard Frankie cry out. Then she took the phone away from him.

"Mama, mama, can you hear me?"

"Yes. Sweetheart. Now give the phone back to the gentleman."

Frankie cried. She called her uncles and they all cried from the joy and relief of finding Ella. "Uncle Shane, we are going to take her to the hospital as soon as we pick her up."

Uncle Shane shook his head. "How are they going to put her in the helicopter?"

"They'll put her in a basket and bring her up into the helicopter."

Shane Gregory shook his head. "No, they can't do that. She's terrified of heights. Someone will have to be in the basket with her."

"That's right. I'll tell Storm he has to get in the basket with her," she said. Frankie turned her head and looked at Ash. "Tell Storm he has to ride in the basket with Mama."

Ash lowered the basket, then called Killian back. "Storm will have to ride with her. She has a fear of height."

"Okay, Storm, did you get that?"

"Yep. Hello Miss Ella, I'm going up with you. All you need

to do is close your eyes. I'll hold your hand and keep you safe."

"Thank you, how did you know to look on the mountainside?"

"Your daughter and your brothers told us this is where you would be."

"They know me so well."

"Did you get a look at the men in the vehicle? I'm assuming someone tried to grab you."

"Yes, I saw them. Those men followed me from the city. I thought it was my imagination, so I pulled over to take a breather. I was so tense, I only wanted to relax for a minute. I had worked myself up; my body shook. I felt sick to my stomach. I was so frightened. As soon as I climbed out of my car, they pulled in next to me with tires squealing. I knew they were after me, so I didn't waste time greeting them. I jumped over the small rock wall and ran. I fell down a few times but kept going. I told myself, if you think you have pain now, wait until they get you. I said to myself, that's when you will feel genuine horrible pain," she recounted. She looked around at them. "I believe they were following me. What I'm saying is I think they were going to kidnap me. I would like to hire your company to guard me. I've felt for a while now someone has been watching me."

"Let me check you over, Ella," Storm said as he looked at her hand.

"Are you a doctor?"

"I was a medic when I was in the Seals."

"My husband was a Navy Seal. He was on a covert operation when he died saving his men's lives."

"I'm sorry. When was that?"

"Francis was five."

"So you don't call her, Frankie?

"No. My brothers started calling her that. I'm the only one who calls her Francis. Have you met her?"

"Yes, we found her yesterday, on the mountain. She was looking for you and had fallen and broken her leg."

"What, my Francis broke her leg? Then why is she in the helicopter?"

"She's your daughter. You would know more than I how stubborn she can be. I have no idea why she's here. Our company is all ex-Navy Seals. Does this hurt?"

"Yes. I think I have a broken shoulder, and my hip hurts. I might have broken my hand too. My last fall was pretty bad. I was so frightened. I didn't know how far those men followed me. They chased me for a while," she wiped a hand across her face, "I don't know how long they followed me. I have money, but I have never thought someone would want to kidnap me for it. One man seemed familiar. I've been racking my brain for answers to where I've seen him. These protein bars are delicious," she said as she opened another one and took a drink of water.

"Time to get on the basket," Killian said as he picked her up again. "You can tell Ash to pick me up after he refuels. I'll be waiting. I'll have some men meet you at the hospital, and they'll bring some papers for you to fill out," he told her. His phone rang. "Yes, she's on her way. I'm having some men meet her there. I'll speak to you when I get to the hospital. That was your brother. They are on their way to the hospital. Storm will stay with you until some of the team arrives."

"Thank you."

Storm arranged himself in the basket. It was a tight fit. Then Killian handed Ella to him. He held onto her. "I'm riding in the basket with you. Close your eyes, and when you open them again, your daughter will be there."

"Thank you both. I need to hire your company to watch

my daughter as well," Ella said. She scrunched her eyes closed as they started up to the helicopter.

"Mama, I'm so happy to see you," Frankie cried all over her mom, who was also crying.

"Do you want to check your mom on the way to the hospital?" Storm asked. Frankie nodded, and Storm handed her a napkin. She blew her nose and looked at him.

"Did you check her?"

"Yes," she has some broken bones.

"Oh, Mama, are you in a lot of pain?"

"Only a little honey, don't worry about me. I'm going to be fine. I'm just happy to be here with you."

"Mama, I know you are in pain. I broke my leg, and it hurt like hell. Here…" she dug around in her purse and handed Ella some Tylenol. "We'll be at the hospital soon."

"Killian said to have Ash come back for him after he refuels. Francis, Storm is going to guard you. Those men have been following me, and they wanted to kidnap me. One of them I've seen before, but I can't remember where I've seen him. So I don't want to hear any argument over this."

"Mama, I don't need a bodyguard."

"I will not discuss it right now," she finished. Ella laid back and closed her eyes.

21

Boys, can you please give me room to breathe? Ella Strong looked at her younger brothers. Her father married Jacklyn when Ella was fifteen. And out of that marriage, Ella got three brothers whom she loved so much. But sometimes, they smothered her. Like right now, she was in her hospital bed, her brothers, Killian, Storm, Ash, Rhys, and Frankie were in her room. Frankie was arguing with her brothers. That wasn't anything new. They loved each other so much they tried to smother her as well. They didn't like that she traveled everywhere to operate on small children. Now they were fighting over Frankie having a bodyguard.

Killian tried interrupting. Finally, he walked over and stood in front of Ella. "Shut the hell up. Fuck, I thought my family was loud. Excuse my language, but damn we're in a hospital. I'm sure Ella doesn't want to hear her family shouting at each other."

They looked at Killian and started laughing. Shane slapped him on the back. "This is how we decide things. Okay, Frankie will have bodyguards, and so will Ella. This conversation is over. I want two bodyguards for each woman. It would kill us if something happened to Ella or Frankie."

"Killian walked outside with Storm and Rhys. You two can guard Frankie. Ash, you and Austin can stay with Ella. I'll tell the hospital director and make sure he understands why you're here. I'll go with Frankie until you get a bag of clothes. Then we'll relieve you every week until we find these guys. I had a call from Marc. He and his sister Mandy will be moving here soon. He said he needed to get her away from New Orleans. She has been having nightmares about the killings. When he gets here, we'll work with him. I also have some other ex-Seals who are going to be showing up. Look, we need someone to keep track of where everyone is. Who wants to volunteer for that?"

No one said a word. Storm looked at everyone. "Why don't you be the one to set up the schedule? I'm not good at stuff like that. What about you two?"

"Hey, I don't want to do schedules," Ash said. "You have always been good at shouting orders."

"Well, thank you for saying I'm bossy. I'll take care of the schedules, and I'm having some contracts made up. Jonah can handle all the legal stuff. The Seal house will be our base, anyone who needs to live there can. It has eight bedrooms," he announced. Killian took a deep breath. "Well, go pack bags. I have paperwork to do."

"MAMA, I DON'T NEED A BODYGUARD."

"Francis Marie, you're going to have a bodyguard."

"Mama, even if I don't want one?"

"Yes. Why wouldn't you want these handsome men watching over you? I'm not old enough that I don't know what a hot guy looks like. Listen to me, Francis. I want you to be careful and stay alert. If I hadn't noticed those men following me, I would most likely be dead right now."

"I know. It scares me when I think of those bastards following you. Uncle Shane wants me to stay at his guest house on the property. He won't take no for an answer. I swear you gave them too much power regarding me when I was growing up. Now I'll be where all three of them live. I know it's two thousand acres, but it's on their property."

"Well, I'll be living in James' house, so I'll also be on the property as well. I'm thrilled about it. I don't want to be alone at my place. I'm still so frightened to death. Besides, your uncles are only a few years older than you are. It's not like you're staying with senile old uncles. Shane is only three years older than you. So do you need to go home and pack a few things?"

"Yes," she bent and kissed her mom. "I love you, Mama."

"I love you too, sweetheart."

Frankie went to the door and looked at Storm. "I need to pack some things. We'll be staying at the guest house on my uncle's property."

"Okay, I'm ready when you are," Storm didn't want to spend more time around Frankie. *Damn, I'll continuously be adjusting my pants.* He looked over at Rhys. "Ready?"

"Yep."

Frankie was having a heck of a time walking on her crutches. Her leg hurt, she needed to take a pain pill, but they put her to sleep, so she had to wait until she got home. "I took a taxi to the hospital. Do either of you have a vehicle here?"

Storm took her arm to help her walk. "I have the SUV. You can ride in the back seat. He watched as she tried to walk down the slope. He scooped her up and handed Rhys her crutches.

"You don't have to carry me. I can walk."

"I know you can. This will take some pressure off your leg. Relax and shut your eyes."

"Why would I want to shut my eyes?"

"Because it distracts me when I look into those beautiful green eyes of yours."

"Oh," Was all she could manage. Frankie didn't know what to say to that. She laid her head on his shoulder and closed her eyes. If she was honest with herself, he made her nervous being this close to him. She would always think of him as her rescuer.

"I'm surprised they didn't keep you in the hospital."

"They tried. My friend picked me up after I had my cast on. I wish my mother would have mentioned she thought someone followed her for the last couple of months. We could already have caught them. And mom said she thought she recognized one of them as someone she knew. I wish she could remember him."

"You don't have to worry about anything. We'll get them. I'm sure if those men are so hard up for money to kidnap her, then they'll try again. You have your eyes opened," Storm said, looking into her eyes.

She smiled. "Yes, I know."

"We're at my vehicle, anyway," he uttered. He clicked a button, then opened the back door. He sat her inside, then walked around and fixed her leg as it rested on the seat. "I'll drive carefully, so there won't be any bumps."

"Thank you."

Storm could still smell her scent after he put her in the back seat. She smelled like flowers and vanilla mixed. Damn, he became hard just thinking of her scent. He didn't know how he would last working with Frankie, walking around with a damn hard-on all the time. They first went to her house, which was a condo on a lake. It overlooked the water and was beautiful. She had children's drawings all on one wall. She came out of her room, frowning.

"What's the matter?"

"Someone has been in my home. Someone moved the things on my dresser around," she replied. Frankie hurried as quickly as she could on crutches to the kitchen and opened the second drawer. She pulled out a box and opened it. Inside was jewelry.

"You keep your jewelry in a kitchen drawer?"

"I just received this box when my mom became missing. These belonged to my grandma. My uncles gave them to me for my birthday."

"When was your birthday?"

"Two days ago."

"Happy birthday."

"Thank you. I'm ready if you are."

Storm walked into her bedroom and got her bag. He didn't like the idea of someone coming into her home and going through her things. *I wonder how they got in here.* He walked through the house, making sure everything was locked up. "How do you think they got in here?"

"I don't know. No one has a key except my mom and Uncle Shane. I wonder if the man my mom recognized works for my uncles."

"What do your uncles do?"

"They're cattle ranchers. They also have lots of horses. So they hire a lot of men. I'll call my Uncle Shane and let him know about someone getting in my house."

"Your uncles are young. Did your grandfather remarry late in life?"

"Yes, Shane was born when my mom was at college. They are all one year apart. James is my age. When he was twenty, my grandpa and their mom died in an avalanche in Colorado."

"That's too bad. How old was your grandpa?"

"He was sixty-three, and Millie was forty-eight. They had a marriage of love. My mom said her mother wasn't a good wife. She was a hard woman without a heart," Frankie stopped talking. Her face felt like it was on fire. "I'm sorry. I don't know what has come over me. I never talk so much. And I never tell anyone about my family's life story. It must be the pain pills I'm taking.

"That happens a lot to me. I'm a good listener, so people always talk to me about themselves."

"What about you, Rhys? Do people talk to you like they talk to Storm?"

Rhys laughed as he glanced at Storm. "I can't say I've had anyone I've just met tell me about their family. But you've been through a lot these last few days. When I met Storm, I was a kid of twenty-three. He knew my life story and never opened his mouth. I think people are drawn to him because he's easy to be around. I told him he would make a great psychiatrist. He would never have to open his mouth."

Frankie chuckled. "At least it's not just me. How come your parents named you Storm?" she asked, looking at the back of Storm's head.

Storm shrugged his shoulders. "The night they conceived me, there was a raging storm going on outside. My mom told me she told her boyfriend if she became pregnant, she would name her baby Storm if it was a boy or a girl."

Frankie felt like crying for the little boy who asked his mother how he got his name, "What happened to her boyfriend?"

"A tree fell on the house that night, and it killed him."

"Do you believe that story?"

"Why wouldn't I? My mom never lied to me."

"Do you have brothers or sisters?"

"I do. I don't know them much. I lived with my grandparents after my mom married Pete."

"Well, all I can say is they missed out on a great son and a wonderful brother," she remarked. Then she wiped tears from her cheeks.

Storm laughed. "How do you know I would have been a great son and brother?"

"I've known you for three days, and I already know you would be. I'm not saying any more about it."

"I TAKE IT ALL BACK. You would not be a great son or brother! Why do I need to have you with me all the time? It's been two weeks, and no one has threatened to take me. I want to go to the movies with my friend Jas. I've known her since I was in grade school."

"I don't care how long you've known her. You will either have Rhys or me with you at all times. Why do I have to tell you that every day?"

"Because I don't like having someone breathing down my neck all the damn time. You know I'm going to Australia to do surgery on that little boy, don't you? Are you going with me then as well?"

"Yes, I'm fucking going with you everywhere. I will not argue with you over this anymore. Why don't you just be like your mom and accept it?"

"Because my mom doesn't have to be with someone so hateful all the time. I want you to switch with Austin."

"You got it."

Frankie's chin trembled, and that angered her even more. "Good!"

Storm called Killian. "Hey, Killian, change spots with me and someone else."

"Why!"

"Because Frankie doesn't want me here. She's tired of arguing with me."

"Again, what is this the fourth time?"

"It's the fifth. Put Jonah or Marc over here. I'll trade with one of them. That way, she can't keep changing places with Austin and me."

"Can you put her on the phone?"

"Yep," Storm said then he walked to the other room and handed Frankie the phone. "Killian wants to talk to you."

Frankie took the phone. It was warm from Storm's hand, holding it. She put it to her ear. "Hello."

"Hi Frankie, this is Killian. I want to make sure you want to have another team member guarding you before I move Storm out of there."

"Yes, I can't stay with someone who doesn't allow me to do anything on my own."

"You know that's why he's there, don't you?"

"I don't care. I want someone else." She didn't say it was because she was becoming attracted to Storm.

"Okay, I'll have them there in an hour. You can put Storm back on." Frankie handed Storm back the phone. "Storm, I'll have Marc there in an hour," Killian said.

"Okay, I will not let her change her mind this time. Send me far away."

"You got it. I don't get it. You are the easiest guy on the team to get along with. Why can't she get along with you?"

"It isn't her or me. It's because she isn't used to anyone telling her what to do. She wants to go to the movies. I told her we would go with her. She didn't like the idea of Rhys and me going to the movies with her and her friend. She thinks because it's been two weeks, no one will try anything. Frankie told me the kidnappers have changed their minds."

"Hey, I'm sorry, man. You can go home when Marc shows

up. Your next assignment starts Friday in New York. I'll fill you in when you get here. Marc's sister Mandy is at our house. Bird is showing her around the college. I go home tomorrow. So I hope like hell, Frankie doesn't change her mind again."

"It won't matter. I'll be on the other side of the country."

An hour later, Marc showed up. Storm had his things packed and was filling Marc in on what was going on when Frankie walked out. "Frankie, this is your new guard, Marc Breaux."

Marc put his hand out, and Frankie shook it. "I thought Austin was trading places with you."

"No, it's Marc. Marc, Rhys can fill you in on anything else," he replied. Storm turned toward Frankie. "Bye, Frankie."

"Where will you be?"

"I'm not sure. New York, I think."

"New York. That's so far away. What if I need to talk to you?"

"Frankie, what's going on?"

"Nothing is going on. I just thought you would be at James' house with my mom."

"Get my number from Marc. If you want to talk, call me anytime."

"Goodbye, Storm."

He threw his bag in the back and drove away, calling himself every name he could for not just changing places with Austin as he had been.

Frankie was in shock. She didn't think Storm would go on another assignment. What if that kidnapper came back? Storm wouldn't be here to protect her. She was an idiot. This was all her fault. Who knows, maybe it was better this way. She was fighting the feelings she was having for Storm. Frankie knew it was because he rescued her. That's what it was, hero-worship because he was so strong and beautiful. She let herself think she had feelings for him. Now she could let her heart settle down and forget about Storm. *I don't even know his last name.* She hurried into the house and to her room. *What is the matter with me? I need to get out of here for a while.*

"Hey Rhys, I would like to visit my Uncle Shane if you and Marc don't mind. What is Storm's last name?"

"Anderson, Storm Anderson."

Storm Anderson, that's a good name, Frankie said to herself. "Why don't we walk? The weather is perfect."

"Let me tell Marc, and we'll all leave together."

22

"Killian, someone is here to see you."

"Who is it?" Killian asked, walking out of his home office. Bird shrugged her shoulders. "Rowan, Kane, I wondered if you two would get back to me. It's good to see you guys," he greeted. He looked at Bird. "Sweetheart, these two are a couple of my buddies from the service. Rowan Scott and Kane Walsh. Gentlemen, this beautiful woman is my wife, Bird."

Rowan looked at Bird. "I met you before, at Jonah's. You're Jonah's sister."

"I remember. You both were on leave, and you came to Jonah's house."

"Yes," he replied. He looked at Killian, "We are here to sign up for the band of Navy Seals team."

"Great, we've been so busy. Let me know if you hear of any more ex-Seals who need work. We can use all the help we can get. I never realized how many people need help. We specialize in bodyguard security. So you have to have a license to carry a gun."

"I have my license," Rowan said.

"I have mine also," Kane said.

"Good, then let's get these papers filled out and you can go to the Seal house and stay if you don't yet have your own place. Jonah is there this week. We take turns staying there. Sometimes we have clients there if they are hiding from someone."

For the rest of the afternoon, Killian went over what the team was about. "They hire us to guard them with our lives. If this isn't for you, I understand. You don't have to join."

Rowan nodded his head. "I knew what is involved already because Austin told me everything about the team business. I'm ready to sign on."

"I'm also ready," Kane said. "Jonah also told me everything about the company."

"Good, just sign these papers, and you're a part of the team. I have some documents for you to read. And please read them. It tells you all about our team and what is expected of us. It's good to see both of you."

"It's good to see you again also, Lieutenant. We thought you were dead."

"I almost was a few times, but I'm still alive and kicking, as you can see. I'll see you in a couple of days. I'll call Jonah and let him know you'll be there. Welcome aboard, men."

"Thank you," they both said at the same time.

As soon as they left, Killian's phone rang. "Hello, Frankie, what can I do for you?"

"Killian, I want Storm back. I don't feel safe unless he's here."

"It's been three weeks. Aren't you used to Marc yet? Rhys is still there. Why don't you feel safe with him? He's been there from the beginning."

"I don't know. I know it's stupid. I just miss Storm. I'll call him that might help."

"Yes, call him. He asks about you every time we talk. I told him you were getting along fine with Marc. You don't want to make a liar out of me, do you?"

"No. I'm sorry for calling again," Frankie chuckled, "I guess I miss fighting with him. Bye, Killian."

"Goodbye, Frankie."

Bird walked back into the room. She sat on Killian's lap. "The kids are taking a nap. Mandy is in my office taking all the calls. Why don't we go take a nap?"

Killian picked her up and held her close to him, and kissed her. "Let's hurry before the kids wake up," Killian said. He walked her to the bedroom and laid her on the bed. He took her dress off and ran his hands over her breast. "You are beautiful. I could make love to you all day long."

"Then you better get busy. You know that daughter of yours doesn't take long naps."

Killian laughed and stripped out of his clothes. They were making love for the second time when they heard the doorbell. "Who the hell is that? They're going to wake the kids," he growled. Bird giggled as Killian hurriedly put his clothes back on. "Get dressed, darling. We have company," he added. Killian went to the front door and answered it. When he opened it, Zane Taylor stood there with a smirk on his lips. "You can take that look off your face. Come in. What are you doing in Temecula?"

"I heard the Seals team are hiring."

"You're not a Seal."

"Not now, I'm not. But I was a Seal seven years ago."

"How come I didn't know that?"

"I don't tell people. It was another time in my life."

"You're a DEA Agent?"

"I quit."

"Damn, Zane. You are full of surprises."

"Tell me what happened with the Seals?"

"I got injured underwater, and I freaked out. I quit the

DEA because I can do more for people when I'm not working for the government."

"Okay, follow me."

Bird walked down the hall. "Zane, are you staying the night?"

"No. I'm going back to Arrows. Brinley is making Mexican food."

"She is. Killian, let's go to dinner at Arrow and Brinley's tonight. You know she cooks enough to feed an army."

"My brother is an army. But let's go. I'll call after I give Zane some papers to fill out," he told him. Killian didn't ask Zane anymore about his time as a Seal. Maybe one day he would tell him, and perhaps not. Everyone is entitled to have some things not known by others. "Welcome aboard, Zane."

"Thanks, Killian. It's going to be good working with you."

That night, Killian and Bird lay in bed after making love for most of the night. Killian's hand ran up Bird's inner thigh making her moan in pleasure. "I love you, Bird, more than I thought it was possible to love another human being. Thank you for loving me and being my wife."

"I love you, Killian. I wouldn't want to ever be, anyone else's wife. You are the only man I will ever love. Now can you please make love to me again?"

THE END

FOR A BONUS EPILOGUE OF KILLIAN
CLICK HERE

https://dl.bookfunnel.com/bk7o2lg5pn
Follow me on BookBub
https://www.bookbub.com/profile/susie-mciver

Keep reading for more of (Band of Navy Seals)

ROWAN

23

Rowan kicked back in the sand and took a long swallow of a much-needed ice-cold beer. The only thing about relaxing for a long time was that the image of Piper Campbell would pop in the forefront of his mind as if out of nowhere. Piper was his best friend all through grade school, high school and part of his college years. His regret of losing her friendship and love left a pain in his chest. He could still see her long blonde hair flowing down her back and those beautiful gray eyes that looked like they knew everything he was thinking. He rubbed the spot around his heart and closed his eyes. It was happening again. His heart thumped uncontrollably in his chest every time he thought of her. She was beautiful and smart, and she laughed all the time. Her laughter echoed in his head as thoughts of them doing everything together raced through his mind. They went to all the baseball games his dad got tickets to. She was practically his only movie plus one and she never went to the mall unless he was tagging along.

He screwed up big time with Piper. His friends always wondered why he didn't take her on a real date. They couldn't understand with her as beautiful as she was why he didn't make her his girlfriend. Rowan didn't want to ruin their friendship, that was his reason. He was stupid. When he thought back to the conversations he used to have with Piper, Rowan cringed. God, he would tell her about his dates with other girls. Now he wondered if he hurt her even back then. Talking about how he wanted to take out different girls.

Rowan realized how much he loved Piper when he brought Kat home from college. He was going to be graduating in two weeks, but they made a quick trip home because Kat wanted to meet his family. Now he wondered if she just wanted to meet Piper, who he talked about every time he opened his mouth. Piper finished her third year of college that week and stayed at his parent's house for a week while her apartment was being painted. He wondered at the look that came over his family members when he introduced Kat to them. His brother and sister stayed long enough to say hello, then left, saying they were meeting someone uptown. He now knew they tried finding Piper before she got back home. Unfortunately, they didn't get the chance to warn her about Kat. When she walked into the kitchen, her arms full of flowers, her face lit up when she spotted him. Rowan remembered it like it was yesterday. Piper screamed and threw her arms around him. She smelled like sweet flowers and fresh air. Rowan hugged her back, and it hit him right then how much he loved her. His heart took a dive to the pit of his stomach. What had he done? He loved Piper. She was the only woman he would ever love.

Sure she was his best friend, but Piper was so much more. He always missed her while he was away at school. He talked to her on the phone for hours. He felt like someone punched him in the gut when he thought about what he had done. Then that horrible voice behind him brought his attention back to where he was in his parent's kitchen. And the woman he promised to marry stood with his parents, his brother and sister had just walked in through the back door that was still open.

"So this must be your little friend Piper. Why Rowan, the way you talked, I thought she would be more boyish. Why, she doesn't look anything like a tomboy, and she's not little at all. She's only about five inches shorter than you."

Rowan took Piper's hand. For the first time since he'd known Piper, she pulled her hand loose and stepped back. Kat stepped up to him and put her arms around his waist, "Are you going to introduce me to Piper?"

Rowan watched as his brother and sister stood on either side of Piper. "Piper, can I talk to you privately, please?"

"You don't need to tell her privately. I'm Rowan's fiancée, Kat. I know you two have always done everything together, but as you know, that will have to stop now that he'll have a wife. No more talking on the phone for hours, no more weekend getaways. He'll be doing everything with me now. You'll have to find you another best friend."

"Kat, don't ever speak for me. Piper, can I please talk to you privately?" Piper just stood there staring. Her body stiffened, and she raised her head high. The look on her face broke his heart. He wanted to tell her he made a mistake. That it was her he loved, had always loved, since she was five. He wanted to ask for her forgiveness for touching another woman. He felt guilty. He felt dirty. He took Piper's hand and walked into the other room. Kat followed.

"I was going to wait before I told Rowan my news," Kat's mean ugly voice called out loudly for everyone to hear. He wondered why he never noticed before how her voice sounded. "We are having a baby. I'm so excited. Rowan, do you have anything to say?"

"What? How can you be pregnant? We always took precautions."

"Why don't we let Rowan and Kat talk alone?" his father said, leading all of them out of the room. That was the last time he saw Piper. She left before he could see her. He found his mom and sister crying in the room Piper had just vacated. He knew then, the only thing he had ever enjoyed with Kat was sex. Rowan realized too late how experienced she was. They had nothing else in common. He tried for months to find Piper, but she was finished with him. He joined the Navy and became a Navy Seal.

His good friend Killian Cooper new everything about Piper. Rowan got drunk once and spilled his soul. Rowan figured since Killian already knew about Piper, he could talk about her whenever he felt like talking about her. Sometimes he would talk about her to Arrow and Brinley, Killian's brother and sister-in-law. Rowan told them stories about when they were little, and she would sneak over late at night because she was scared. He never wondered why she didn't just wake her parents up. Later he found out they had gone out to a party or something. They thought since Piper was asleep, they could go anywhere for a few hours. They seemed a little bit strange to Rowan, but then again, what did he know.

He imagined Piper was married with kids by now. He used to call her and leave messages on her phone. He told her how sorry he was, and how much he loved her. She never called back. Rowan never mentioned her to his family. He was ashamed about the way he hurt her. He hoped she was happy wherever she was. He was taking another drink when someone kicked sand all over his legs. He looked over at his brother, Colin. "Do you have to do that?"

"You were looking like you wanted to punch someone. You're not allowed to be grumpy on this trip. Here comes

Shannon. I thought for sure she would be asleep by now. She hasn't even been to bed yet."

"I heard that. I'm having all the fun I can have before I have to go back home to those little terrorists for kids I have."

"Sweetheart, they are not terrorists. They are normal boys. Isn't that right, Rowan? I'm sure you and Colin were just as wild as our boys are."

Shannon laughed, "Rowan wasn't wild. He had Piper as a friend. She kept him calm. Colin, on the other hand, was a wild child. I remember when he got in trouble climbing over our neighbor's fence after throwing our dog's favorite toy over there. He was in trouble when my dad found out that he stepped on Mrs. John's prize flowers."

"Shannon, you can't remember anything. Piper threw the toy over the fence, and who do you think gave me a lift up over the wall? It was Piper."

Rowan froze at the first mention of Piper he'd heard from his family. Suddenly, he threw back his head and laughed, remembering he watched from his window as Piper helped Colin over the fence. They were the same age. They must have been eight at the time. Piper told his dad to hit her if he felt like hitting anyone. "Do you remember Dad's face when she told him to smack her and not Colin? Piper said it was all her fault. That's when she started taking care of Mrs. John's flowers, and her love for flowers grew. Everyone on our block had flowers all over in their yards. She would find a spot and start digging. She didn't even tell them what she was doing." Rowan paused and a welcoming smile graced his face. "Wow, I haven't talked to you two about Piper since the last time I saw her."

"We knew how emotionally upset you were about everything. We never wanted to bring her name up to you, and you never mentioned her. You two were so close. Piper said it took a long time for her not to call your number and share something with you."

Rowan used to think Piper was lonely, but how could she be? The entire block loved her. Her parents were always doing their own thing. He remembered once hearing her mom telling his mom they were surprised when she became pregnant with Piper. They never wanted children, and then after twenty-five-years, she was pregnant. She was almost fifty when Piper was born. When Piper turned eighteen, they sold their house and moved to Florida. Piper went to a state college close by, and her parents bought her an apartment in town. For some stupid reason, Rowan used to think Piper would always be in his life. He was a jerk.

"Piper's parents died in a boating accident a few months ago. Their bodies were never found. The boat blew up. The authorities said it must have had a gas leak and someone lit a cigarette or something," Shannon said, looking at Rowan whose eyes were now bulging in astonishment. She knew he loved Piper and Piper loved him. Everything changed that day eight years ago when Rowan brought that lying bitch Kat home to meet the family. Piper sold her apartment and moved away. She brought so many laughs to their house, and then she was gone. It seemed like forever before she came back.

Rowan looked at his sister and frowned, "How did you know about her parents?"

"We went to their funeral."

"Who did?"

"All of us."

"Are you saying you've stayed in contact with Piper all these years?"

His brother looked at him like he was crazy, "Piper is like family to us. Why wouldn't we keep in touch with her?"

"Where does she live?"

"She lives in Mrs. John's home, some of the time. She left it to Piper in her will."

"Are you fucking kidding me? The only woman I have ever loved lives next door to my parents and no one thought to tell me."

"When do we see you? Piper moved back home last spring. She's remodeling the house right now but goes back and forth to Florida. She's keeping her parents' home on the beach there."

"What does she do?"

"What do you mean?"

"What kind of work does she do?"

"She's the owner of Piper's Flowers."

"As in The Piper's Flowers."

"Yeah, they're all over the United States. She's famous. Shannon looked at him and shivered. She told me she had a stalker and had to get a restraining order against him. He would write her sick love letters, and it scared her." Shannon leaned over and whispered, "She bought a gun."

"Does Piper know how to use a gun?"

"I don't know." Shannon looked over at her husband, who was a detective, "Does she know how to shoot a gun?"

"No, I tried teaching her, but she shuts her eyes before she fires and always misses the target. She said she will threaten him with it if he ever comes around her again."

"Are you telling me this guy has followed Piper back to Northern California?"

"I'm not sure if he followed her there or not. She had someone looking in her kitchen window when she was eating dinner one night. It could have been a peeping tom.

"Has she never married?"

"No, never. God, she doesn't ever want to go through that pain again," Shannon whispered under her breath. "She's been too busy building her business."

Colin turned and looked at him. Rowan knew he was angry, he saw it in his clenched jaw, "Why the hell are you so worried about Piper now? You haven't seen her in eight years. You were with that bitch, and broke Piper's heart. I don't think you should get involved in Piper's life again. You don't know how much you hurt her. We do."

"I'm not going to get in Piper's life. I'm concerned about her. I know how crazy people can be. If we knew the guy's name, I could have him checked out."

"Henry already had him checked out."

Rowan looked at his brother-in-law, "What did you find?"

"Nothing, the guy had gotten into a little trouble when he was a teenager, but that's all there was. We couldn't find anything else."

"What's his name? I have a friend who can find everything from the time he was born. If there's something he's done, she'll find out what it is."

"His name is Samuel Brown. He's from Portland, Oregon."

Rowan picked up his phone, "Hey Brinley, can you check someone out for me?"

"I thought you were on vacation."

"I am. The guy's name is Samuel Brown from Portland, Oregon."

"That sounds more like a user name. Are you sure it's his real name?"

Rowan looked at Henry, "Did you guys take his fingerprints?"

"No, we never came into contact with him. The restraining order was written up in Portland. Piper lived there for a few years. I don't even know what he looks like except what Piper has told me. She says he's about six feet with brown hair and brown eyes. I'm sorry I'm not much help. I called Portland to send me his photo, and they never did. Piper said she has his picture on her phone."

"They took his fingerprints in Portland when the restraining warrant was issued." He turned the conversation back to his phone call, "Brinley, if you could please do this for me, I'll owe you."

"You already owe me. But since Arrow is out of town, I have some spare time on my hands. Who put a restraining order against him?"

"Piper Campbell. If you get a photo, can you send it to me?"

"Wait, are we talking about The Piper Campbell?"

"Yes, I wish I never talked to you about her. Please don't mention her to Arrow or Killian."

"I promise. Okay, as soon as I find him, I'll send you everything. Does Piper still live in Portland?"

"No, she's back in Northern California. She said she saw him looking in her kitchen window."

"Have you talked to Piper?" Brinley asked excitedly.

"No. I'm vacationing with my family, and they told me."

"Oh, darn."

"Brinley. Stop it."

"Well, it's been eight years. Can I tell anyone about this?"

"No!"

"Okay, okay. I guess my lips are sealed then. I'll call you. Keep an eye out for an email."

"Thank you."

As soon as he was off the phone Shannon asked, "Who is Brinley?"

She's Killian's sister-in-law. She married Arrow Cooper. Do you remember me telling you about Killian? He was my Lieutenant?"

"Yes, he was lost on an island for a year. Who did he marry?"

Rowan smiled, "He married Bird."

"Bird, someone named their daughter Bird?"

"Birdine, she doesn't like that name, though. Sometimes she comes to the Seal house with Killian. You guys would like my friends."

"I don't know. I mean, they all sound a little on the rough side. They've actually killed people."

"You're married to a detective. I'm sure he's killed someone before."

"No, I've never had to shoot anyone. Where we live, it's nice and quiet."

"Then what do you investigate?"

"Well, we have had killings. No place is perfect. I just haven't shot anyone."

24

Piper could feel someone looking at her. She panicked and ran out the back door and through the gate Colin put in last month, so she could walk over to his parent's house from her backyard. Piper stopped running, she couldn't take that crazy person over to the Scott's house. Shannon and Henry's children were there. She turned around and ran back into her house. Piper's lips trembled as she walked into the kitchen. *I have a gun. I'll take it out and scare anyone who tries getting in my home.* She knew as soon as she locked the door, it was too late. He was in there with her. Piper could almost feel him breathing down her neck. The hair on her arms stood up. She was so scared she thought she would die. Piper was glad she didn't run over to Mazy and Fred's house. This guy was not nice. She knew who he was. He would have followed her to Mazy's. Piper prayed she had the courage to go through whatever came her way. That's when she heard the laugh. It scared her so much she ran as fast as she could, but he grabbed her hair and pulled her back.

"You belong to me, Piper, the flower lady. The second I

saw you with all those flowers in your arms, I knew you belonged to me. All this beautiful long hair belongs to me. Everything about you belongs to me." He started smelling her hair and kissed the back of her neck. Piper cried out, her knuckles turned white, her fist was gripped so tight. "Don't make me angry, Piper Campbell. I had to kill another woman, and I'm trying really hard not to kill anymore. My father would have me put away again if he knew what was going on. My real name isn't Samuel. It's Frank. My old man is a Senator. Well, he's not my old man, he's Troy's. He takes care of everything I do. Except for the first time he had me locked away for five years, and I was only thirteen."

"I don't give a damn who your father is. I am not yours. Get out of my house right now," Piper barked as she brought her foot down hard on the top of his foot. He slugged her in the face, and she fell down.

"Did I forget to tell you I enjoy beating women?"

Piper picked herself up from the floor. Her nose started to bleed. She grabbed a towel and put it over her nose.

"I love to watch the blood flow from someone's body. It makes me hard. Let me see the blood flow from your nose."

"Kiss my ass, fucker." Piper ran for the back door, but he caught her.

"Well, then I'll cut a different spot on you and watch it bleed. I should have been a butcher," he laughed and dug his fingernails into her arm.

"No, please don't," her voice shook when she begged for her life, "Why are you doing this to me? I've never done anything to you."

"You took a restraining order out on me. My father had to take care of that, and I can tell you he wasn't happy. He ordered me to stay away from you. That was a big mistake! No one will keep me away from you. Who the fuck does he think he is ordering me around. He can't tell me what to do.

I'll do whatever I want, and right now, I want to see blood coming from your body."

"No," Piper yelled as he took a sharp knife from his pocket and made a slice down her neck. He started making weird noises and humping his body against her. Piper gagged as he licked the blood from her cut. She almost vomited as he held her hard against his pelvis and began to play with himself while he sucked at her neck. She cried out when he grabbed her breast and squeezed it hard. Suddenly, he started moving faster, and he cried out like he was in pain. Then he laughed while he rubbed his hands over her body. He tried to put his hand down her pants, and she kicked him and scratched his face. Piper fought like hell to keep him away from her. What was she going to do? Colin, Shannon, and Henry were away on vacation with Rowan. The boys were over at Mazy's. She had to keep him away from their house.

"Stop fighting me," he shouted as he backhanded her.

"No. I will keep fighting you until I take my last breath. Why would you think I wouldn't fight you? I'm not ever going to let you touch me if I can do anything about it."

"Don't you understand you belong to me? There is nothing you can do about it. I will do anything I want to you, and you will end up dying because all your blood will be gone. See, it still drains from your neck as we speak."

Piper raised her hand to touch her neck, and he let out a piercing scream, "Don't touch your neck. That belongs to me. He jerked her to him and started sucking hard on her neck. Piper thought she would die. The pain was so intense his teeth were biting into her as he sucked. Piper felt tears wet on her cheeks. Then he licked her face. He pulled her top up and tried to lick her breast. Her knee slammed into his groin. He fell to the ground, and she took off. He grabbed her foot. "No!" Piper cried. "Leave me alone, and get out of my house."

"Shut the hell up! You know, I was going to let you live longer than I did the other lady, but you are starting to be too much trouble. Stay still, damn it, or I will kill you and then drain your blood."

Piper had to think. She had to find a way to get away from this psychopath. Piper knew he would kill her, but if she could talk her way out of him doing it so fast, maybe she could escape. "Why do you want to kill me?"

"I don't want to kill you. But I have to kill you. If I don't, then David gets angry and makes me do worse things."

"Who's David?"

"Don't ask so many questions," he shouted. *'Stop yelling at Piper. She didn't do anything to you.'* "Yes, she did. She wanted to know who David was. You know he will become angry if I don't do this." *'Let her go. David is all talk. He won't hurt you.* Are you crazy?' *"Yes, I am. I have all of you living in my head, so that makes all of us crazy."*

Piper knew right then that this guy was a schizophrenic. He had all these people talking at once. She hoped to hell David didn't come out while she was with him. He should be in a mental ward. He wouldn't let go of her foot.

"Hi, my name is Troy. I want you to know I won't have anything to do with killing you or drinking your blood. I'm going to stay around to make sure David doesn't show up."

Piper looked at him and nodded her head. She had to keep Troy on her side. She had no idea what David would do, and she didn't want to know.

"I'm hungry, so I'm going to tie you up and get something to eat," Troy said, looking around for something to tie her with. He pulled the lamp out of the wall, cut the cord, and tied her so tight she couldn't move. Then he tied her feet.

"Why don't you let me go before Frank or David shows up?"

"Because bad things happen when I go against them.

There are more of us. Paula, you would like. She doesn't like David or Frank, but she's afraid of them too. The baby cries the entire time she's here. I don't like her coming out. She keeps hunting for her mommy, and she can't find her."

Piper was thinking, if the baby came out, at least she might have a chance of getting away. *Fuck, he's making me as crazy as he is. What am I going to do?*

25

Rowan's phone rang as they sat on the sand. He picked it up and looked at the screen. "That was fast."

"Where does Piper live?"

Rowan told her the name of the town. He could hear Brinley clicking away at the keys. "What the hell is going on?"

"His name is Troy Broan. He's schizo, he has many other characters, and they all live inside him. David and Frank are the killers. Troy was locked up for five years when he was a teenager. His father is Lou Broan. He's a Senator who has nothing to do with his son. I have some men going to Piper's house. I hope to hell she's there. I'm calling Arrow. He's up in that area right now."

Rowan broke out in a sweat, "Fuck, fuck, fuck." By now, he was pacing. His family was up walking next to him. They all looked worried. "I'm leaving right now."

"What!" Colin demanded to know.

He talked as he rushed back to the hotel, "The man who is after Piper is a psychopath killer. He's schizo and has many men living inside of him. Two are deadly killers." He got on his phone and called for a plane. "Pack fast. I have a plane waiting. What's Piper's phone number?"

Colin pulled out his phone and dialed her number. There was no answer. "Use my phone," Rowan said. Colin punched it in and waited. Still no answer.

Henry called the police station. "Have a few of your men go check on Piper..." He went on to explain what was going on.

~

"TROY, you know if I don't answer the phone, then whoever is calling me will come and check on me."

Troy turned away from the bacon and eggs he was cooking and put his fingers to his lips. He pointed to his head. That was enough to scare Piper.

"If they keep calling, answer, but don't give anything away. David will go to your neighbors and kill them as well."

Piper would give anything if she wasn't tied up. How is she going to get away if she can't run? "Can I please go to the bathroom?"

Troy took a deep breath and turned around, "You are trying my patience, flower lady."

She knew Frank was back. Tears welled up in her eyes. Nausea swept through her.

"If I let you go to the bathroom, then I get to cut your breast and suck the blood out."

"You are a sick bastard."

"I know that honey, but better me than David."

"Where's Troy?"

"He's gone, now. Do you want to go to the bathroom or not?"

"No."

"I didn't think so." He took a bite of the eggs and bacon. His mouth was smacking as he chewed. Egg yolk ran down his chin. Piper turned around and ignored him. She glanced at the clock. It was already eleven-thirty and pitch-black outside. Her phone rang again. He got up and held the phone to Piper's ear.

"I'll let you answer it, but one false move and David will be here."

Piper nodded her head. It was strange how each one had their own voice. He pushed the button. "Hello,"

"Piper?"

Piper wanted to cry. Why was Rowan calling her? She hadn't heard his voice in eight years. "Yes."

"Do you know who this is?"

"Yes."

"Are you alright?"

"No." The phone went dead. "Why did you turn it off? I haven't talked to Rowan in eight years. I thought he loved me, but he broke my heart. I wanted to see why he was calling?"

"How did he break your heart?"

"He met someone in college and asked her to marry him. They were never married. His sister told me all about it, whether I wanted to hear it or not. Kat was her name. That is one name I never liked. She pretended to be pregnant. I haven't seen him or talked to him since the night he introduced me to Kat, his bitch of a girlfriend."

"If he calls back, you can ask him why the hell he broke your heart."

Piper raised her head and looked at Paula. It couldn't be anyone else. She had a woman's voice.

"I'm Paula."

"I thought you must be."

"I'm sorry about all this. If I could help you, I would, but

David would go whacko and start killing so many people. That's what he did the last time Troy tried to help someone. I hope that jerk calls you back. Why would he want someone else? I've watched you since Frank started stalking you, and you are kind. I see how many people you help. If I wasn't in this body, I would be just like you. You're beautiful without wearing all that make-up. You aren't all high and mighty even though you are famous. Troy's father thinks he is high and mighty. He makes me sick. Troy feels the same as I do. We haven't seen him in years."

Piper was struggling to keep up with everything she was saying. She jumped when her phone rang. Paula pushed the button and held it to her ear. "Hello."

"Piper, Sweetheart, why did you hang up on me?"

Piper looked at Paula, and she rolled her eyes. *What can I say to let Rowan know I need help?* "Rowan, why are you calling me? I don't want to talk to you."

"Then talk to Colin." He handed the phone to Colin, "Piper, are you at home?"

"Yes, I'm here. Colin, can you do me a favor? Call your Mom and Dad and tell them to go to Shannon's house right now. Will you do that?"

Colin looked at Rowan. They both knew Troy was with Piper. "Yes, I will. Are you okay?"

Shannon picked up her phone and called her Mom. She told her to get out and go straight to the police station.

"No. I love all of you." The phone was thrown across the room, they heard a loud scream before David smashed the phone.

Piper was out cold. When she woke up, she was in the back of a car. Her brain was a little fuzzy, and then it all came back. David was let loose. He had her, and they were going somewhere fast. She thought she heard sirens and realized it was her ears ringing. They sped down the

Highway at an alarming rate of speed. The car was swerving all over the road. He made a U-turn and hit something hard. The car was now out of control. Piper didn't dare say anything. She could hear muttering in the front seat.

Frank and David were arguing about turning themselves in. "Troy's dad will get us out. He always does." *'FUCK YOU! This is your fault because you became an idiot over this woman, now I will take care of her.'* "No, you won't. She's mine. You will keep your hands off her." *'Pull this car over right now. You are not going to cut her up. She belongs to me.'*

"I don't belong to anyone!" Piper screamed as she threw herself at the driver of the car. She put her arms around his neck and with her hands still tied, she tried to choke him. "Stop this car right now and let me out." She saw the clock on the dash board and couldn't believe it was three in the morning. She put her hands over his eyes and tried to make him wreck the car. If they wrecked, at least she had a chance. Her breathing came out in long deep breaths. He grabbed her hair and pulled, hard. She couldn't think. Finally, she got her hair loose from him. She knew she was the only one who could save herself. If David or Frank got her, she would be dead. Piper saw an SUV come up next to the car she was in. The guy pointed for her to get down, so she took her arms away from the crazy man who wanted to kill her and got on the floor. She heard glass break, and the car swerved. It went off the road and hit a tree. Piper didn't move until someone opened the door. Next thing she knew, she was lifted up and out of the car. Someone carried her up the bank and sat her in the back seat of the SUV. She raised her head and looked at the man who smiled at her. He had long black hair tied back off his face.

"How do you feel," he asked as he untied her hands and feet.

"I'm okay. Are they dead?" Her feet were tingling, and her face hurt.

"They," he raised his arm immediately and pointed a gun at the car down the bank. Arrow didn't know there were two men.

"Troy, Frank, David, Paula, and the baby—I never met the baby. Troy is a schizo. He wasn't the one who killed the people. Paula was okay. David killed lots of people, and Frank was going to drain my blood and drink it when he killed me. See my neck." She couldn't stop talking.

Arrow looked into her eyes. "Who hit you?"

"Frank, the last one was David. It must have knocked me out. Because I remember it was eleven-thirty now it's three in the morning. Who are you?"

"Arrow Cooper, Nice to meet you, Piper Campbell."

"Do you know me?"

"No. I've never met you." He smiled like he had a secret.

"I'm glad you showed up when you did."

"You can thank my wife for that. She can track anyone with her computer. She's a bit of a whiz."

"A friend told her you left your house. I was just pulling into town to check on you when she called. She tracked his car on satellite."

"Who is your friend?"

Arrow didn't want to answer that question, but he had no choice. "Rowan Scott."

"Rowan Scott," Piper shook her head, and a sorrowful look came over her. "He called me tonight. I wonder how he knew Frank was at my house."

"He had Brinley check out who was stalking you. When she found out who the guy really was, she got worried and sent me here. I was in the next town over."

"Are you a cop?"

"I used to be. Now I work with my brother, Killian."

"You killed that man, and you're not a policeman. Won't you get in trouble?"

"I was saving your life. I had no choice but to shoot. I'm taking you to the hospital to get checked out. Rowan's mom is there waiting for you."

"Okay. Thank you." Piper stared ahead. *Why does Rowan have to come back into my life? I won't allow it.*

Arrow buckled her in, and she leaned back and closed her eyes. Arrow looked at her as she slept. He didn't think she even knew she had those cuts on her arms and neck. He knew why Rowan couldn't get her off his mind. Piper was not only beautiful. She had sweetness flowing from her. He knew it upset her when he mentioned Rowan's name. He could see the pain in her eyes. When he pulled into the hospital parking lot, he saw a woman standing outside, looking around. He stepped out of the car, and Piper opened her eyes. He walked around to help her from the vehicle. When she stepped out, her legs buckled, and the woman ran over as fast as she could.

"Piper, sweetheart," she looked at Arrow, "thank you for saving her. I was so worried you wouldn't find her."

"You're welcome. I feel like I've known Piper forever."

"I wonder why you feel like that," Piper remarked.

"Because Rowan has told us all about you. From the time you were five-years-old. My wife is on her way here. I hope you don't mind. She was coming up to stay with me for a few days, and she wants to meet you."

"She does?"

"Yes, she just realized that Piper's Flower's and Rowan's Piper Campbell were the same person. I'm afraid I won't be able to keep her away."

"Does she have a flower business?"

"No, Brinley is an FBI special agent."

"Wow... Wait, I feel strange. I think I'm going to faint."

And that is what she did. Arrow carried her into the emergency room as two officers walked in to get a statement. "You're going to have to wait on that. Piper is in no condition to answer questions right now."

"We'll ask Piper questions later. We have questions for you."

Mazy Scott sat by Piper's bed as she slept. She couldn't believe the nightmare she must have gone through with that man in her home. She heard her telling the police everything that happened. Thank God for Arrow Cooper. She saw someone standing at the door and raised her head. Rowan stood there. Mazy went to him and put her arms around her oldest child. He loved the woman who lay sleeping in the bed. He loved her more than most men could ever love a woman. Mazy knew that because he told her. They walked out of the room and down the hallway.

"How is she?"

"She's frightened. He hit her a few times with his fist and cut her. What a nightmare—the guy had all these personalities. When Piper talks about it, she talks as if there were four different people."

Piper screamed. Rowan and Mazy ran inside the room. Rowan knew she was having a nightmare. He pulled her into his arms and held her. His mom walked out. He was thankful she did. He had to wipe the tears from his eyes. Her face was swollen from that bastard hitting her. She had five cuts where he sliced her with a knife. He gently laid Piper back on the pillow. That's when he saw her neck. His mom walked back in. "What the hell happened to Piper's neck?"

Mazy pulled him back over to the door. "Frank, he was one of the bad guys in the man's head, cut her throat, and sucked her blood. Piper said he bit her while he sucked. That's what he did with all her cuts. That's how he was going to kill her while he was doing horrible things to her."

~

Piper didn't want to look at Rowan. She didn't understand why he was here. Sure, Brinley and Bird were his friends. She liked them, and just because they were here didn't mean he needed to be here too. Of course, his parents lived next door, and maybe he was at their house most of the time. That was one thing about living by this family. She loved them like they were her own family. She was with them more than she was with her parents growing up. Piper was always worried Rowan would move back to town. She watched him out the window as he walked around her backyard, talking on the phone. He looked the same and yet, somehow, he looked different. He was all grown up, his shoulders were broad, and she didn't remember him being so tall. He had whiskers on his face. He looked tired, like he needed sleep. She didn't want to take her eyes off him. She loved him so much. *Why do I still have to love him?*

Piper didn't know he stayed at her house at night because of the nightmares she kept having. Or that he slept next to her most of the night. Bird and Shannon cleaned up the mess in her home. They took out the broken furniture that broke when she was fighting for her life. Shannon didn't want Piper to see the broken table or the blood on the towel and on the floor that came from her. She lost a lot of blood from her cuts. Besides the cut on her neck, there were five other deep ones. Rowan thought Piper must have been knocked out when those happened because she had no idea she had them until she woke up.

Rowan walked around Piper's back yard in awe. She put so much work into what she did back here. Piper always put hard work into anything she did. Rowan used to think she did it to get attention from her parents, but it didn't work. No matter how hard she worked, they still didn't notice her.

He looked at the rock, and the pond seemed so natural. The fish looked like this was their natural home. It was beautiful, as was his parents' backyard. Rowan was pretty sure the entire block got a redo in their yards. That was the kind of person Piper was. He knew why she was the famous Piper Campbell who Brinley told him about. After Rowan found out she was his Piper, he googled her. He watched every YouTube video he could find and looked on as she laughed with strangers who threw their arms around her, excited to meet her. He watched her surprise people in hardware stores with complete redoes of their backyards. Rowan laughed out loud when, in a video he was watching, a man picked Piper up and swung her around as his wife jumped up and down, clapping her hands. She volunteered to do work for seniors who could no longer take care of their property. She hadn't changed at all. He loved her, but he didn't know how to explain to her what he should have told her eight years ago.

Rowan didn't claim to be without guilt. He'd been with women. He'd never been with anyone for more than a couple of months. He wasn't interested in having a relationship with anyone. He loved Piper. He tried getting over her, but it was useless. He loved her and would continue until he took his last breath. Rowan knew it wouldn't be fair to another woman, so he never let anyone inside his world. He kept things as casual as he could and was very upfront about it. He never thought he would see Piper again. All the times he'd been home, Piper hadn't been there at the same time, nor was she ever at her parents'. Though his family never brought her up, Rowan didn't know why he thought they hadn't seen or been in touch with her. They were always so close. He was so ashamed of the way it ended with her that he never thought to bring her up himself. He never believed she would want to see him, and he was right. He acted like a punk sixteen-year-old who had sex for the first time. He was only with Kat for a few weeks before he "proposed" and only a few months when he took her home. She was the one who insisted on it. When he had time to think back on it, she was the one who decided they would get married. He was an idiot who let his dick lead him down the wrong road. He wasn't thinking with his brain until he saw Piper, and his world crashed down around him.

PIPER WAS in the garden sketching a layout for Brinley's backyard when Bird told her a man wanted to see her. She came into the living room to meet him. When she saw the man, she knew right away who he was. The Senator looked just like his son. Piper felt the blood drain from her face, and she broke out in a sweat. She knew Rowan stood behind her. Piper could feel him. She felt stronger knowing he was there.

"How can I help you, Senator?"

"You know who I am?"

"You look like your son," it was Brinley who answered as she walked into the room.

"Brinley, how have you been? It's been a while since we've seen you around Washington DC. I'm happy to see Miss Campbell has friends with her." He looked at Piper, "I came to tell you how sorry I am. I know Troy's people in his head think I covered for him. But if I knew where he was, I would have made sure he stayed locked up. I didn't want them to let him out the first time. He convinced his sister that he was normal, and when she took him in, he tortured her. She committed suicide. I didn't know she let him move in with her. My daughter was a bright, sweet twenty-five-year-old." A deep sadness played on his face and he seemed to be somewhere else in his thoughts for a moment. He spoke again, looking directly at Piper, "I only wanted to tell you I'm sorry."

Piper walked over and took the Senator's arm. She could only imagine how much pain he was going through. "Let's have a cup of tea." She led him to the table and put out home-made cookies, and made each of them a cup of tea. "Troy didn't want them in his head. Have you ever talked to any of them?"

"No, I haven't talked to Troy in ten years. He'd been in hiding."

"But he said you warned him to stay away from me."

"I definitely didn't speak to my son. When they called me to tell me he was dead, it was the first time I heard about what he'd done to you. I'm not surprised that he would say that though. He knows I would have been extremely upset and would have gotten him into a facility had I known what he was doing." The senator gave a long, hard sigh.

"It wasn't his fault. It's the illness," she offered him some comfort. "Frank and David were the evil ones. The strange thing was they all had their own voice. It was like different people were arguing. I wasn't scared of Troy or Paula, even though they were afraid to help me. They tried keeping Frank and David away from me. I'm glad he's gone because, otherwise, I would be dead."

They talked for a while longer, Piper as much heart-broken for the Senator who'd lost two children as she was upset for herself and what she'd only just been through. The Senator left shortly after taking a phone call.

"Well, that was unexpected," Piper said, looking at Bird and Brinley, then her eyes landed on Rowan. "Why are you here?"

"Because I want to keep you safe. I love you. I'll always love you. I wanted to tell you that day, but I never got the chance."

"I haven't seen or spoken with you in eight years. Are you crazy? You don't know me. You know the child that I used to be. I'm no longer that foolish young girl with rose-colored glasses on. I'm a grown woman who doesn't want to talk to you." She threw her hands in the air and turned around, then she turned back and spoke to Rowan. It hurt seeing him standing in her kitchen, even after all these years. "God, why did you come here? Do you even know how hard it was for me?" Tears rolled down her face. Her fisted hand pressed against her heart. "I can't do this. Not now, not ever. I promised myself I would never allow another person to have control over my feelings. I've worked hard getting you out of my life and my heart. Please don't make me go through that again." She left without waiting for his response and walked upstairs to her room. *I don't need to be here while the house is being renovated. I have to leave and fix myself again. I need to deal with what happened to me. I won't let myself lean on another person. This is my responsibility. I'm the only person I have.*

"ARROW AND KILLIAN have finished their business, and they'll be by to pick us up early in the morning."

"I'm going to miss you and Bird." Piper gave Brinley the blueprints she made for her backyard.

"Piper, how can I thank you. I'm so excited to get started on this project."

"Where did you say you live again? I might know of someone who can do the work."

"We live in Temecula."

"Oh, yeah, Temecula. I have a warehouse there."

"I know, that's where I get my plants."

"I know the perfect person." Piper paused as if thinking, then she added, "I'll call him and set up an appointment with you. It's strange, I have a house in Temecula. I'm surprised we haven't run into each other there."

"I've seen you once or twice. I just didn't say hello for fear you'd think I am some crazy fan. Which I am by the way," Brinley gave a slight giggle and Piper responded with a bright smile. "We've only lived there a year, though. But we love it."

Piper didn't want to ask this question, but she had to. "Does Rowan live there?"

"No, he lives in Los Angeles. Their company has a huge home there. If he's not there, then he has a home in the hills somewhere. I've never seen it, but I've heard it's beautiful."

"What is their business?"

"High security, bodyguards, among other things. They do a lot of rescue work as well."

"I have a present for you, Piper," Bird said, walking in with a large box that wasn't staying still.

"Oh my, what's in here?" Piper said as she lifted the lid off the box. Inside was a beautiful Chocolate Lab puppy. She was suddenly overcomed with emotions. The puppy jumped from the box into Piper's arms and she cuddled her close. All of a sudden she began to cry. "I'm sorry," she said, sniffling. "You must think I'm a fountain as much water that comes from me. I love her. I've always wanted a puppy, since I was little. Rowan used to promise to get me a puppy when I no longer lived with my parents." Piper didn't know why she had to bring that up, "What's her name?"

"You get to name her."

"I do." She looked into the puppy's eyes, "Okay, let me look at you. Umm, this might take a while. Do I need to do it right now?"

"No, you can name her when you find the right name."

"Have I thanked you two for staying with me this week? It was nice having someone to talk to. It's going to be nice having the puppy with me. She's the best present I've ever had." She hugged Bird. "How did you know I wanted a dog?"

"Everyone should have a dog for company."

KILLIAN BOOK 1

My Book

ROWAN BOOK 2

My Book

ZANE BOOK 3

My Book

STORM BOOK 4

https://www.amazon.com/dp/B08Y7C9D4Z

ASH BOOK 5

My Book

JONAH BOOK 6

My Book

KANE BOOK 7

My Book

AUSTIN BOOK 8

My Book

LUKE BOOK 9

My Book

RYES BOOK 10

My Book
FOLLOW ME ON SOCIAL MEDIA

Newsletter Sign Up http://bit.ly/SusieMcIver_Newsletter

Facebook Page: www.facebook.com/SusieMcIverAuthor/
https://www.bookbub.com/profile/susie-mciver
https://www.susiemciver.com/
https://www.goodreads.com/author/dashboard

Printed in Great Britain
by Amazon